Dare to Surrender

Dare to Love Series #3

Invitation to Eden Multi-Author Series

NEW YORK TIMES BESTSELLING AUTHOR

Carly Phillips

Author's Note

Dare to Surrender is the story of my heart. I wrote the first 100 pages during a very down time in my life, when I was losing my father, with whom I was very close. I needed an outlet – a book that I didn't owe to anyone. One that reflected the types of stories I love to read along with the challenge of first person point of view. Then of course, the characters of Isabelle and Gabe grabbed me and wouldn't let go. When I was given the opportunity to join in the Invitation to Eden series, I knew immediately this was the chance to finish Isabelle and Gabe as well as to give the Dare siblings some cousins. And Dare to Surrender was born. For those who have asked if Dare to Surrender's first person point of view means the rest of the Dare series will be in first person too? NO. Ian and Alex and their siblings will be in third person. If there is a good response to Dare to Surrender, Gabe's siblings, Lucy and Decklan will get their stories too – but those will be in first person. In other words, please leave reviews, email, and let me know! And now I hope you love Isabelle and Gabe as much as I do.

Dedication

To the Invitation to Eden Authors – You made me feel truly Indie. I love the adventure and I'm proud to be in this with you all. Thank you to Janelle Denison (Erika Wilde) for … everything. And a special thank you to Lauren Hawkeye for coming into my life and brightening it … a lot!

Dare to Surrender
by Carly Phillips

PDF Edition
CP Publishing 2014
Cover Design: The Killion Group Inc.

carlyphillipsauthor@gmail.com
http://www.carlyphillips.com

Sign up for Carly's Newsletter
http://www.carlyphillips.com/newsletter-sign-up/

Sign up for Blog and Website updates
http://www.carlyphillips.com/blog

Sign up for Text Updates of New Releases
http://tinyurl.com/pbq4fbx

Carly on Facebook
https://www.facebook.com/CarlyPhillipsFanPage

Carly on Twitter
https://twitter.com/carlyphillips

After ending a relationship to a cheating, domineering man, Isabelle Masters takes off in her leased Mercedes, only to be arrested for grand theft auto and hauled to a local police station. To her surprise, she is rescued by the most unlikely person possible, Gabriel Dare, a man she's been attracted to for far too long. Gabe offers Isabelle freedom along with an invitation to Eden, an exclusive island resort where everything and anything is possible.

Although Gabe yearns to possess Isabelle, he knows all too well he must fight his primitive need to bind her to him, and instead help bring out the independent woman she yearns to become – or risk losing her for good.

A woman who needs to run her own life. A man who needs to exert control. Can she surrender to his erotic demands without losing her sense of self once more?

**A unique story connected to both the DARE TO LOVE series and INVITATION TO EDEN. This book can also be read as a stand alone.*

* * *

Invitation to Eden

We are very pleased to issue your Invitation to Eden, an exciting series coming to you in 2014 from 27 of the biggest names in romance. Join us as we take you on an exciting adventure to Eden, where anything… and everything goes!

www.invitationtoeden.com

Carly Phillips

Prologue

Gabe

Gabriel Dare eyed the beautiful woman with the bright smile that didn't reach her eyes, hoping his bland expression concealed the intense emotions she roused inside him. Protective instincts the likes of which he'd never experienced before. The desire to sweep her into his arms, breathe in her unique scent no designer could have created, and steal her away from this god-awful staid country club was strong.

He had an endless supply of beautiful women all eager to share his bed, including Naomi, his latest affair, and yet they did nothing for him except accompany him on endless nights like this one. And take the edge off his need. True satisfaction hadn't existed for him in far too long.

He was bored. Unless he was watching *her*. Then

the perfection and elegance of the Hamptons club vanished, and *she* was all he saw.

Blonde hair fell down her back in less-than-perfect waves, defying the stick-straight look most women preferred. Her lush, sexy body, so unlike the females he normally bedded, had his hands itching to learn those curves and show her what true pleasure really was. She was unattainable, living with one of Wall Street's stars, but she could do so much better.

Oddly, it wasn't her lack of availability that appealed. She was bright, witty, and she could hold her own with just about anyone, making whoever she spoke to feel important. He admired that trait. They hadn't spent more than a few minutes here and there in each other's company, but she'd taken his breath away from the first look.

Gabe would do just about anything to attain something he wanted, but he drew the line at poaching on another man's territory. Still, he had to admit she tested even his willpower, and he'd had practice at being alone. He'd married young and miscalculated badly. Afterwards, he'd been certain that after Krissie's death, for which he felt responsible, the smart thing would be to keep a safe emotional distance from women.

One look at Isabelle Masters and he'd changed his mind. There was something about her that filled the emptiness inside him. To the point where just watching her was enough to calm his usually restless soul. Unfortunately, they didn't run into each other nearly often enough.

Gabe ran a hand through his hair, groaning as he caught sight of Naomi making her way toward him, a cocktail plate with one celery stick and a carrot in her hand. His gaze darted to Isabelle as she crossed the room in the opposite direction, careful to avoid him as long as the man she lived with was around.

She was taken, and all he could do was admire. Look and not touch. But if she ever became available, all bets were off.

Carly Phillips

Chapter One

Isabelle

He begged me not to walk out the door. I did it anyway. The scariest part? How much I wanted to go. I'd spent years of my life fully invested in a relationship I'd thought meant everything to me. How could all the emotion disappear?

The answer came to me as I stood in the dark driveway by my car, the only light coming from the headlights of the vehicle I'd turned on with the push of a remote. The feelings had drained away, diminishing slowly from something I'd hoped would be full and wonderful at the age of twenty-two to something painfully empty by the time I'd reached twenty-five. I wasn't old, but at this moment, I felt ancient and weary down to my bones.

I glanced up just as the first drop of rain touched my face. Normally I'd pull up a hood and protect my out-of-control curly hair from frizz, worried about how I'd look to Lance and the carefully chosen people with whom he surrounded himself. He called them friends, but none knew the meaning of the word. Instead, I embraced the wildness of the storm that suddenly threatened to release from the heavens. Each warm droplet hit and spread across my cheeks, cleansing my skin and my soul. The wind took flight, lifting my hair, blowing strands onto my face and setting the rest of me free.

"Isabelle!" Lance yelled down from the window he'd opened on the second floor of his Hamptons summer home. It had been too long since I'd considered any part of it mine. If I ever had.

I unwillingly looked up.

"You've had your tantrum. Now come back inside, and we'll talk like civilized people. You don't want to cause a scene in front of the neighbors."

Heaven forbid, I thought, sparing a last glance at the place I'd lived for too long. The house was Lance Daltry's showplace, just as I had been nothing more than an accessory. I may have organized his personal life and thrown obligatory dinner parties, but I'd contributed nothing of substance. He'd never allowed me to spend any of the money I'd earned before I'd quit my interior design job. Unnecessary, he'd said. If I loved him, I'd stay home and take care of the house.

More like he'd wanted control, and I'd given it to him.

Luckily for me, I'd saved a good amount from those early days. Not so luckily, I'd let Lance invest my money and maintain control of those accounts. And what were the chances that money would be available for my withdrawal on Monday morning? I closed my eyes at the thought.

Although I'd been in Manhattan for a couple of years by the time I'd met Lance, I was still the naïve girl who'd taken a bus from a small town near Niagara Falls and traveled to the big city alone. Too bad I hadn't had the street smarts to peg Lance for the phony he'd turned out to be.

"Isabelle!" He yelled down to me again, not bothering to come out in the rain to talk to me, let alone apologize like a man. Not when the rain would ruin his thousand-dollar suit and hundred-dollar haircut.

Not talking, I thought silently, and merely shook my head.

Talk was what had gotten me to remain in a relationship I knew I didn't want with a man I couldn't trust; it was what had convinced me that Lance, a Wall Street trader, was my soul mate when, in the deepest part of my heart, I knew there was no such thing. And most humiliating, talk was what had led me to believe his lies, despite knowing I wasn't truly satisfied with him or in his gilded cage.

I didn't need therapy to tell me why I'd been so susceptible to Lance's charm and desire to own me. The childhood I didn't like to think about held the answers. But having escaped him now, one thing was certain. I wasn't going back.

"Would you quit being a child and get back here!" Lance tried once more, patronizing me even though he was the one in the wrong. Another favorite ploy of his.

Shaking, I climbed into my beloved car, slamming the door and escaping Lance's tirade. I started the engine and paused, breathing in deep, the events of the last few minutes rushing through my brain like a bad film.

I'd been on our shared laptop, searching for recipes I'd stored there. Seeing a file I didn't recognize, I'd clicked. And the graphic, sexual images of a naked and sweaty Lance along with my beautiful neighbor, who'd dared to call herself my friend, had flashed on the screen. Nausea had risen at the visual proof of what I'd only suspected before.

I shivered at the memory of those images, proud of how I'd walked out without a word—or a suitcase. My body was frozen, my heart encased in ice. Although I could turn on the heated seats, the reminder of what it felt like to be numb with betrayal would keep me safe in the future.

I turned on the ignition, but surprisingly, no water

works mixed with the dampness from the rain. Instead, adrenaline raced through my veins faster than even my beloved car could take a highway. I ought to be afraid. Panicked. Yearning to turn around and go back to the security I'd known.

My foot pressed the accelerator, and I backed out of the driveway without looking back. I might not know where I'd go or what I'd do, but I was moving forward. At last.

On the satellite radio, the 1980s Bugles song proclaimed that video killed the radio star. *Untrue*, I thought, as I drove into the dark night. Radio had thrived anyway. And tonight, though video killed my dream of living happily ever after in a life I thought I'd carefully crafted to prevent loneliness, those graphic sexual images of betrayal wouldn't destroy me. Instead, they'd set me free.

* * *

Isabelle: Out of the Frying Pan

I was arrested a mile outside of Manhattan. Grand theft auto, the cop said. Bullshit, I replied. The baby Benz belonged to me.

Still, he cuffed me and hauled me to the nearest police station. He said his name was Officer Dare, and he was a dark-haired man, tall, taller than Lance, who prided himself on his height, and broader beneath his uniform, from what I could tell. His intense expression never wavered. All seriousness, all the time, but I sensed he'd be handsome if he smiled. So far, he hadn't.

Once inside the typical-looking police station—not that I'd seen the inside of one before, but what I'd thought one would look like from watching Law and Order—he sat me beside his wooden desk and *cuffed* me to the desk.

I ought to be scared, but some stupid part of me had already decided this new part of my life was some grand adventure. At least it was until Officer Dare asked me to empty my pockets and divested me of my last five hundred dollars, cash I'd taken from the *extra* stash I kept in my nightstand.

He thumbed through the bulging stack of twenties in never-ending silence.

The money represented my lifeline. "I'll need to eat when I get out of here," I told my jailer.

He didn't look up. "You'll get it back."

"All of it?" I asked as if I seriously believed a member of the police force would take a *down-on-her-luck* woman's chance at food.

He set his jaw in annoyance. "We log it and count it. In front of you. I was just about to do that … ma'am."

For some inane reason, I burst out laughing. I'd gone from living in denial to homeless and arrested in a ridiculously short time. This whole turn in my life really was absurd.

I rubbed my free hand up and down over one arm. "Don't I get one phone call?"

He nodded and reached for the telephone on the desk.

I frowned, suddenly realizing I had no one to call. Lance was out of the question, and *our* friends were really *his* friends. As for my parents, they didn't remember my birthday, so something told me a late-night call to pick up their daughter from jail would not be their number-one priority.

"Never mind," I said softly.

The officer stared at me, confused. "Now you don't want to use the phone?"

"No thank you." Because I was totally, utterly alone.

Nausea rose like bile in my throat, and I dug my nails into my palms. When I forced myself to breathe deeply, the familiar burning in my chest returned, and I realized I'd walked away without the one thing I never left home without, and it wasn't my license.

"Any chance you've got some Tums?" I asked.

He ground his teeth together, and I swear I heard his molars scraping. "Okay, yeah. I'll get right on that," he muttered and strode off.

"I'll just wait here," I called back. I lifted my arm the short distance the cuffs would allow and groaned.

What felt like an endless stretch of time passed, during which I reviewed my options, of which, once again, I had none.

Now what, I wondered, utter and complete despair threatening for the first time. Eventually I forced back the lump in my throat and forced myself to make the best of the situation.

I kicked my feet against the linoleum floor. Leaned back in the chair and studied the cracked ceiling. Hummed along to the tune crackling on the radio in the background. And yeah, I tried not to cry.

"You know, I thought it would take me longer to get you in cuffs." A familiar masculine voice that oozed pure sin sounded beside me.

It couldn't be, I thought, but from the tingling in my body, I already knew it was. "Gabriel Dare, what brings you into this part of Mayberry?"

He chuckled, a deeply erotic sound that matched his mention of the handcuffs, but he didn't answer my question.

Left with no choice, I tipped my head and looked into his self-possessed, dark blue eyes. Eyes too similar to my cop, and suddenly the last name registered. In an unfamiliar place and time, my mind on my arrest and nothing more, I hadn't made the connection before.

I knew Gabriel Dare from the country club Lance belonged to, but despite the upper-crust connection, there was nothing similar about the two men. Where Lance was sandy-haired and a touch Waspish in looks, Gabe, as his friends called him, possessed thick, dark sable hair and roguish good looks.

Gabe's very posture and demeanor set him apart from any other man I'd met. His white teeth, tanned skin, and chiseled features were put together in a way that made him extraordinarily handsome. That he owned the space and air around him merely added to his appeal. An appeal that had never been lost on me, not even now, shackled as I was to a desk in a police station.

His stare never wavered, those navy eyes locked on me, and if I hadn't been sitting, I'd be in a puddle at his feet.

"You look good cuffed," he said in a deliciously low voice.

Immediate thoughts of me bound and at his mercy assaulted me. My body, which hadn't been worshiped well in far too long, if ever, had been taken over by the notion of Gabe, his strong touch playing me with an expert hand.

I squeezed my thighs together, but instead of easing, the ache only grew. Heat rushed through me at a rapid pace, my breasts heavy, my sex pulsing in a dull throbbing that begged to be filled. I blinked hard in an impossible attempt to center myself.

He grinned, as if he'd heard every naughty thought in my head.

It had always been this way between us. Any time I ran into him at the club, the attraction had been electric, and when we found ourselves alone, the flirting, outrageous.

One night, Gabe had caught me exiting the ladies' room. Lance had come upon us then, and once home, he'd accused me of desiring Gabe. I'd denied it, of course.

I'd lied.

Lance knew it, and after catching us talking privately at more than one event, he'd kept a firm lock on my arm. And because I desperately wanted the life I'd chosen to make sense, I'd allowed the possession.

Besides, Gabe always had an elegant woman on his arm, a different one each time. He could have any beautiful female he desired. Why would he choose me? Even Lance, who I'd been with for what felt like a lifetime, liked ownership, not *me*. And let's face it, my parents hadn't wanted me either. So believing in myself wasn't my strong suit.

"So. What are you in for?" Gabe settled in his

brother's chair, propping an elbow on the cluttered desk so he could lean closer. "Prostitution?"

"Excuse me?" I choked out. "You know I'm not a hooker!" I said, offended, the whispers I'd heard when Lance and I had first gotten together rushing back.

Gold digger and *mistress* were among the chosen words, never mind that Lance's single-minded pursuit had broken down every one of my defenses.

Gabe chuckled, assuring me he'd been joking. "Seriously, you dress down as well as you dress up." His gaze raked over me, hot approval in the inky depths, appreciating me in a way Lance never had.

My insides trembled at the overwhelming effect this man had on me. "Where's the cop with my money?" I asked, glancing around.

"Worried about your stash?" Gabe drummed his fingers on the desk. "Are you sure you're not a hooker?" he mused.

I didn't want to grin, but I did. "Why are you so desperate to think I am? Are you a pimp or something?"

He burst out laughing, the sound echoing through the walls of the quiet station. "Not quite," he said, obviously amused.

The tread of his brother's heavy footsteps announced his return.

Gabe looked at the other man with a disappointed

expression. "Bro, didn't anyone tell you you're supposed to handcuff a lady to the headboard, not a desk?" He folded his arms across his broad chest. "It's no wonder you can't get any action."

I ducked my head, trying not to laugh.

A flush highlighted the other man's cheeks. "What are you doing here, and why are you bothering my suspect?"

Gabe tapped on his wristwatch. Gold. White face. Rolex. All my jewelry was in Lance's safe, I realized, the thought making me sad. Not because I was materialistic but because some of the pieces, the few I'd chosen myself, I really had liked.

Gabe glanced at his brother. "Didn't you say you were off at eleven? I thought we'd go check out the club I'm thinking of taking over."

"Are you really looking for a new club? Or is this trip an excuse to find some new woman to warm your bed?"

His sibling doesn't pull punches, I thought, glancing away, not wanting Gabe to see my reaction to the thought of any female in his bed.

"I'm still with Naomi."

My stomach still twisted uncomfortably.

His brother frowned. "She's a bitch."

I cleared my throat, unwilling to sit here a minute longer and listen to details of Gabe's love life. "Hello?

Prisoner still here!" I reminded them with a wave of my free hand.

Gabe grinned at me.

I looked away, not wanting to acknowledge the utter rush of pleasure that small gesture brought me.

"What's she in for?" he asked his brother.

"Grand theft auto, but her boyfriend dropped the charges."

Gabe swore under his breath. "That son of a bitch had you arrested?"

I latched onto the latter part of his statement. "Lance dropped the charges?" Relief swamped me, and if I'd been standing, my knees might have given out.

"Charges dropped," the cop restated. "As long as you agree to relinquish the car."

My head whipped up. "That bastard." He was still trying to control me. He knew I'd left with next to nothing, yet he still had to strip me of the one thing he knew I loved. Realistically, however, since I couldn't afford to park my baby in the city, Lance had done me a favor.

"Deal," I said to Gabe's brother. "He can have the car."

"I wasn't negotiating," the cop said.

"Decklan." Gabe's tone held a definite warning.

I didn't need or want Gabe going to bat for me,

and I ignored his hot—and I do mean hot—stare.

"Release me?" I jangled my chain.

Decklan—I now knew my jailer's name—nodded. "Your boyfriend said he'd come down to get you so you two could talk out this … misunderstanding. In which case maybe you can keep the automobile." He glanced at his watch. "He'll be here in about thirty minutes, give or take."

"Oh hell no." I wasn't going anywhere with Lance, and I certainly didn't want the confrontation sure to come if he showed up. I jangled my cuffed wrist, suddenly desperate to escape. I had to get out of here *now,* and I needed a head start.

"Decklan! Unlock the damned cuffs," Gabe barked at his brother in a baritone that ironically settled me.

His officer brother, however, jumped to do his bidding.

I shook out my hand and glanced down. A red stripe bruised my skin, and I rubbed my sore wrist.

Gabe's gaze followed my every movement, his eyes darkening once more. With a low growl, he lifted my hand and stroked my marked flesh with his strong, tanned fingers. A sudden vision of him gripping me harder, pulling me roughly against him, grinding his muscular body into mine, took form, and I trembled, aroused by his tone, his sensual touch, and my torturous thoughts.

"Are you okay?" Gabe asked gruffly.

His voice returned me to my current location and predicament. "Yes. Fine."

An intimate smile curved his lips, and I would swear he knew exactly how hot he'd made me, how wet.

Shaken by the thought and my impending reality, I grabbed my sweatshirt from the chair. "I'm free to go?" I asked, pulling on the light jacket.

"You are," his brother said. "Stay out of trouble, Miss Masters."

I would, I thought, once I escaped his brother. I held out my hand, and Decklan handed me back my money.

"Thanks," I said and winced.

What was next? Gratitude for arresting me?

At least I hadn't gotten as far as the booking process and mug shot. I ran a hand through my wild curls, suddenly aware of how I might look.

"See you guys around," I said on a wave and a forced laugh.

"Wait!" Gabriel's deep pitch almost had me melting toward him again.

"What?"

"Do you have someplace to go?" he asked, too kind for me not to be embarrassed, and I refused to look him in the eye.

"I'll be fine."

"Isabelle—" Gabe's voice deepened.

"Oh no," his brother said. "Absolutely not."

"Shut up, Decklan."

I narrowed my eyes, wondering what conclusion the cop had arrived at that I wasn't privy to. My gaze swung back to Gabe, who merely nodded at his sibling, as if all had been decided.

"You'll come home with me," Gabe said, his tone definitive.

"What?" I hadn't seen that coming, nor could I begin to process the words.

He braced one hand on the wall beside his brother's desk. "You'll come home with me. I have plenty of room, and you can stay till you get back on your feet." His words sounded confident, sure, and obviously made sense, at least to him.

Panic spiraled through me at the thought of going from one controlling man to another.

"Are you insane?" Decklan asked. Loudly.

I nodded, agreeing with him. "Listen to your brother. I'm not going anywhere with you. You're practically a stranger."

Gabe frowned at that comment.

"And she's a stray," Decklan added.

"Hey!" I turned to him and scowled. "That's just

insulting."

"You have a thing for strays," Decklan said to Gabe, ignoring me. Giving me more reason than just my arrest to dislike Officer Decklan Dare.

"Shut the fuck up," Gabe muttered, his jaw set as he glared at his brother.

Decklan had hit a hot button, I noted, and wondered who the stray woman was to Gabe. What she'd meant to him.

I couldn't afford to find out. "It's been interesting," I said on a rush. "Later, boys."

And while the two brothers remained locked in a silent, combative stare, I turned and strode out of the station house without looking back.

Chapter Two

Isabelle: Into the Fire

I'd barely escaped the door of the police station and hit the night air when rain assaulted me, soaking through my clothes almost instantly.

I dove back beneath the awning, where it was dry. Plan, I thought. I needed a plan. I'd left my cell phone at Lance's house, and even if I hadn't, Lance would shut off my service as soon as he realized I wasn't coming back.

I hadn't yet made it into Manhattan, where a taxi would drive by, light on, waiting to be hailed, and I had no ride to the nearest bus or train. I ran a trembling hand through my damp hair, wondering why I'd bolted out of the station when I really had nowhere to go. Even if the rain miraculously stopped, I was all alone.

"Hey."

I turned. Gabe had followed me outside. From the tips of his black shoes up the dark denim jeans that molded to his hard thighs and the white collared shirt open enough to reveal his tanned chest and dark hair, he looked delicious enough to eat. And I wanted a long, thorough taste. I might be panicked and needing to get out of here, but I couldn't deny his appeal.

At the sight of him, a rush of relief washed over me, though I couldn't say why. "You're leaving alone? Did your brother decide the nightclub scene wasn't for him?" I hugged my arms tighter around me. It might be summer, but I was growing colder and more chilled.

He studied me as if he knew exactly how uncomfortable I was, both in my clothes and with myself. He didn't answer my question, merely waited for me to come around to the inevitable—I might not want to be beholden to him, but he was my only option.

I swallowed the little that was left of my pride and met his gaze. "Can you take me to the nearest bus station?" I asked through chattering teeth.

He shoved his hands into his front pants pockets. "So you can go where?"

I swallowed hard. "I'll figure it out when I get away from here, and I need to do that before Lance arrives." I stuck my head into the rain and looked up and down the quiet street, afraid the sound of a car motor would break the silence and ruin my escape.

Gabe grabbed me by the waist and pulled me back under the awning before spinning me around, turning me to face him. My terry cloth jacket hung open, and my nipples, hardened from cold, grew tighter beneath his hot stare. If I peeked, no doubt I would see them poking through my thin shirt.

He looked *there*, saw what I was too embarrassed to do more than imagine, and a vein throbbed in his temple.

"Let's go." He grasped my hand and steered me out into the rain, to the parking lot on the side of the building where a black Porsche 911 Turbo waited.

He unlocked the door, opened it for me, and helped me inside. To my surprise, he popped the front trunk and returned, covering me with a blanket before closing me inside the small car.

He strode around to the driver's side, climbed in, and started the ignition before hitting a series of buttons, turning the heater on, including the one in my seat. I didn't relax until he pulled away from the small police station, leaving any possibility of a confrontation with Lance behind.

I wrapped the quilted covering around me for warmth, and as more distance passed, it slowly dawned on me I was safe. The feeling was so at odds with my normal tense state I almost didn't recognize it. I also understood a big part of that relief stemmed from being with Gabe, something I didn't want to question too strongly at the moment.

Once on the highway heading back to Manhattan, Gabe broke the charged silence. "Is there anyone you want to call?"

I clutched the blanket more tightly. "I have old friends in the city, but I'm not sure they're still living where they used to. It's been a long time." I stared out into the dark night.

"So that leaves you where?" he asked, the kindness in his voice reminding me he wasn't just a stranger I was attracted to, he was a friend. Or could be.

I sighed heavily, hating myself even as the breathy sound escaped. "I don't know. I left a bad situation without thinking things through."

"That much is obvious." One hand on the wheel, he drove with precision and confidence, turning his eyes from the road to face me for a moment. "But you did leave." Satisfaction sounded in his tone. "What were your plans?"

I shivered, and he raised the temperature.

"I thought I'd find a cheap motel where I could hole up and think. Which I still can do since your brother returned my cash."

Gabe set his jaw, much the same way his brother had when I'd said something to aggravate him.

"You're coming with me."

I sighed, the sound heavy in the enclosed space. "It's not smart, Gabe." I didn't need to elaborate on why.

He reached over and covered my hand with his. "Maybe not in the way you mean, but for my peace of mind? Your safety? It damn well is."

I closed my eyes in acknowledgment. The sexual tension between us scared me, but that didn't come close to more immediate fears. I wasn't afraid of Lance tracking me down, but if I were honest with myself, the kind of rattrap I could afford in the city freaked me out.

I wasn't stupid. Gabe was offering me a lifeline. I might not know him all that well, but the way he took control and his dark edge gave me a sense of security Lance never had, not at the beginning, middle, and especially not at the end of our relationship.

Okay, I thought to myself. *Decision made.* "I'll go home with you. For now."

His deep exhale told me my answer pleased him, and I liked having his approval. I narrowed my gaze, confused by the reaction and the warmth rolling through me.

"You won't regret it," he assured me.

A smile curved my lips. "That remains to be seen."

His wry chuckle echoed around us.

He maneuvered the stick shift as if the car were a part of him, the high speed no match for the powerful man. Which made me wonder more about him.

"So what do you do for a living? Besides invest in nightclubs?" I asked.

"Various things."

I rolled my eyes. "Such as?"

"I own hotels and nightclubs," he said.

"It's better than you being on Wall Street," I mused.

"Technically, one of the hotels is on Madison, but I live off the East River."

I whistled before I could stop myself. "Swanky address."

"Decklan picked you up on your way from the Hamptons. Not so rough yourself," he reminded me.

I swallowed hard. "That's over."

Yet here I sat, en route from one man's cushy beach house to another's deluxe apartment. I exhaled and said what I should have from the beginning. "Thank you for helping me out."

"My pleasure, kitten."

The term of endearment sent a rush of warmth skittering through me and a distinct pulsing between my thighs.

"Stay as long as you need."

I shivered at the prospect of being alone with

Gabe. I wished I knew how long I'd need to remain there, but the hard truth was, his generosity would help me get my head on straight and give me breathing room to make decisions about my future.

"If I stay, I need to earn my own way." I was finished being kept by any man.

"So we're back to prostitution after all?" he asked, laughing before I could take offense.

I blushed, my cheeks hot. "I just don't want to take advantage of your kindness."

"I'm not kind," he said, his severe words at odds with the lightness from seconds before. "But if you insist, we'll work something out."

I exhaled in relief. More relaxed now, I leaned my head back against the sturdy leather and closed my eyes, when a very unwelcome thought intruded.

I bolted upright in the seat. "Won't your girlfriend have a problem with me staying over?" Even before I'd been on the receiving end of being cheated on, I drew the line at going after another woman's man.

His gaze slid to mine. "It won't be any of her concern," he said, the words clipped but certain.

"I… Oh." I bit down on the inside of my cheek, not knowing how to respond to that or what he meant.

We remained quiet, only the rain lashing down on the windshield breaking the silence. I shut my eyes and let the steady beat wash over me, lulling me into oblivion.

"Wake up, kitten." A familiar, soothing voice washed over me.

A gentle shake and I came fully awake, my surroundings registering. Gabe's car.

"We're home," he said in the deep voice that caused a flood of moisture between my thighs and a distinct softening of my brain.

The one that told me I was in trouble. Sexy, compelling trouble.

* * *

Isabelle: Home?

I'd assumed Gabe's apartment would be huge. Gorgeous. Expensively decorated. He looked like a man who expected and would only accept the best. And I'd been around enough of Lance's associates to know how the other half lived.

Gabe's place put anything Lance owned to shame. It was a three-bedroom, three-and-one-half-bathroom apartment with not one but four terraces on Fifth Avenue. Yep. Apparently off the East River meant on the *most expensive street in the world.* I was a fountain of useless knowledge, as Lance liked to remind me when I'd occasionally spout out a tidbit or fact I'd learned from the Internet, television, or books.

Something else about me, I'm a bookworm and not the least bit ashamed of it. So when, in the midst of my tour of Gabe's living space, I found myself in a den with fully lined bookshelves and a movable wooden ladder, I instantly fell in love. Not with the man, I assured myself, but with the library.

"You can read in this room anytime you like," Gabe said, pleasure in his voice that I loved his library as much as he obviously did.

"I still don't understand why you're doing this," I murmured. "Your brother is right. You must like taking in strays. How many before me?"

He came to a complete halt in the entryway of the library, a furious look in his eyes, and not one I liked aimed at me.

"None," he said.

We both knew he lied.

With a tip of his head, he started back toward the foyer, past a closed door. "What's this room?" I asked, eager to change the subject, at least for now.

"Bedroom," he said, his tone still clipped. "Come. This way."

I was still thinking about the library and the books, some hardcover, others paperback, all appearing in pristine condition.

"One day I'd like to hear that sound for something

other than books," he said, his tone lighter than seconds before.

"Seriously, what am I supposed to say to that?" It was like the handcuff comment at the precinct.

Gabe chuckled, grasped my elbow, and led me back through the elegant inlaid marble entryway from which I'd entered to the other side of the massive apartment.

"Master bedroom here," he said, pointing to the open door leading to his suite.

I wasn't ready to get an intimate look at his personal space, so I waited for him to move us along.

"And this is your room," he said.

Next to his.

I swallowed hard and stepped inside. Wall-to-wall windows on one side surrounded by light, drapey-looking white curtains, and another generous set of windows on an adjoining wall.

"You can see Central Park in daylight," he said, his tone back to normal. "My sister, Lucy, stays here when she's in town."

"How many of you Dares are there?"

"Three. Lucy lives in L.A. and runs our clubs out there, and she has no visits planned. Feel free to use whatever you'd like until we can get you a wardrobe of your own."

I spun from the gorgeous view to look at the

equally gorgeous man. "I'll borrow your sister's clothes if you're sure she won't mind." I wasn't going to touch his other outrageous statement.

"She won't. Lucy's the most generous woman I know," he said, the warmth in his voice both unexpected and touching.

He seemed pretty generous himself, at least to me.

He swung open the door to what I figured was the bathroom. It was actually a luxury spa, a mix of cream, taupe, and brown marble. The shower was filled with more nozzles and hoses than I knew what to do with, and even a bench inside.

"I'm sure Lucy left enough bottles of female stuff that you'll make do."

I managed a nod. I didn't want to admit I was overwhelmed but was certain he could see it in my face. Channeling Scarlett O'Hara, I decided that tomorrow I'd deal with things in a much better frame of mind.

Chapter Three

Gabe: Revealed

Gabe silently thanked God his houseguest escaped into the shower as soon as she possibly could. The tour of the house had just about done him in. Isabelle's oohs and aahs had been genuine, as had her love of his favorite room in the place. Unlike Naomi, who had taken one look at his apartment and immediately begun calculating how she could move in permanently, Isabelle, who he had invited, not only wanted to pay her way but she planned to leave as soon as possible.

Not if he had his way.

Back at the police station, outside in the rain, it'd been all he could do not to reach out and swipe his hands over her responsive nipples, feel her tremble beneath his touch, and get rid of the ridiculous distance between them. He might not know her well, but he'd always felt they'd connected. The physical attraction was obvious. She was all woman, supple curves, her breasts full and lush, and she possessed one hell of an ass. His cock twitched with desire he'd felt from the moment he'd first seen her on Daltry's arm.

But things ran deeper. They'd shared banter and flirting during opportune moments when he'd caught her alone. He'd had glimpses of the intelligent, witty woman she was when not with that pompous ass. But not until today had he really seen beyond the exterior beauty to the depth beneath. Those sexy blonde curls that bounced wildly around her face were a proud testament to the fiercely independent woman she desperately wanted to be.

The woman he intended to help her find.

It wouldn't be easy. Isabelle needed gentling. Understanding. Patience. Not his best traits, but when it came to her, he'd already exercised plenty. He'd bided his time, knowing Daltry would fuck up sooner or later. The balls that made him a crack financial investor also imbued an arrogance that would be his downfall. And it had been.

It was Gabe's good fortune that Daltry's screw-up had landed Isabelle at his brother's police station. Seeing her there had given him insight he wouldn't have had otherwise. In Isabelle, he saw an intriguing combination of weary life experience and innocent ingenue. It was the innocence the most primitive part of him wanted to conquer, to possess. Since he'd begun running his father's empire at the age of twenty-one, the same age he'd been drafted into surrogate parenthood to his sister, he had always gotten what he wanted.

And Gabe wanted Isabelle.

Chapter Four

Isabelle: Sleeping Beauty

After Gabe left my room, I prowled around, inspecting the beautiful flowered artwork on the walls. Georgia O'Keefe originals if I wasn't mistaken. I'd always been drawn to the bright colors and light. I searched the drawers for clothes, discovering that Gabe's sister and I had similar taste. In fact, we shared some of the same items, but mine were back in my old closet, while hers were lying unused, inviting me to squeeze my Ds into her obviously more compact Bs.

Gabe was right. Tomorrow I'd have to go buy some of my own clothes, and I cringed at the thought of digging into my meager savings but would because I wouldn't let him buy me the way Lance had.

I took a long, hot bath, lingering and feeling ultra decadent as I relaxed into the whirlpool bubbles.

After, I dressed in Lucy's sweatpants, mortified to discover that they, too, were a size too small. Clearly the woman didn't have my boobs or my size ass. And here I'd really wanted to like her.

With a resigned sigh, I stepped out of the bathroom, surprised to find a tray of food at the foot of the bed, a chilled bottle of Bling H20—which cost forty dollars a bottle thanks to the Swarovski crystal-encrusted wording and the champagne-like cork. I knew this because Lance complained when I requested tap water at his favorite restaurant, insisting I order only the best.

And Gabe kept the water in his home. The bottle was too pretty for me to even open. Well, the man did own exclusive hotels and clubs, and I knew he'd been featured in online gossip columns more than once for his single, eligible status. He certainly desired and could afford the very best.

Still, I was thirsty, he had left it for me, and as with most things in my life at the moment, I had no viable choice. I ate the scrambled eggs, not questioning too hard whether he'd made them himself, I was so hungry.

But the biggest impact of the night came from the other item on the tray. The newest Nora Roberts book, hardback, which had just gone on sale this past Tuesday. I hadn't yet ventured to town to buy myself a copy. Now if I'd thought about it, I would have resigned myself to waiting until I could afford it or found a library that was sure to have a long wait list.

Why Gabe owned the book was a mystery. How he'd known that was my taste in novels even more so. Especially since I didn't want to come off as a starry-eyed romantic. Unfortunately, he'd figured me out already. Ready to read and relax for the first time all day, I crawled into the luxurious bed, sinking into the mattress and cuddling into the duvet, planning to read.

Next thing I knew, sunlight, muted by drawn curtains, streamed through the room. I blinked and instinctively knew the light wasn't what had woken me. I forced my eyelids open to find Gabe staring at me from a chair across from the bed.

"Morning, Sleeping Beauty." He sipped coffee while he read the paper, as if being in my bedroom was perfectly normal, something he did every day.

Mortified, I sank deeper beneath the covers. "Get. Out."

He looked me over from head to toe, heat in his predatory gaze. I had to be imagining things. I wasn't vain and was well aware that my hair always looked like a bad eighties perm experiment in the morning.

"What's wrong? You're completely covered," he said, closing the paper.

I blinked, wondering when my world had gone

mad. "I was asleep. That's private! It's first thing in the morning. Why would I want you to see me this early?" I realized I was shrieking and forced air into my lungs, calming myself down. Hysterical shrew didn't become me. "Look, if I'm going to stay here, I want a lock on that door." There. I'd managed to regain control of my voice.

He grinned. "There is one. But now that you've reminded me, I'll have it removed." He folded the paper and set it down on the table beside him.

"This arrangement isn't going to work out." I mistakenly shifted, sitting up higher in the bed, revealing the tank top that barely covered my breasts and pulled too tight where it did.

"Calm down," he said, still clearly amused. "We need to talk."

"And it couldn't wait until I was decent?" My voice rose again. *Modulate*, I muttered under my breath.

"No. It's something that needs to happen now, and I want you here when I teach Daltry a much-needed lesson."

I gulped in air. "Why in God's name would you do that?"

"Any man who lets a woman leave his home in the dead of night with nothing but the clothes on her back, a small stack of bills, and no cell phone deserves it." He cocked an eyebrow my way, that possessiveness there in his blue-black gaze. "That he did it to you merely compounds his error."

I bolted upright in bed, forgetting all about modesty and coverage. "You really need to explain this." I gestured back and forth between us, ending with a clean sweep around his sister's bedroom. "You don't know me well enough to care that much about what Lance did. You can't expect me to believe you'd have taken in just any … stray," I said, pulling his brother's word out for good use. "But you took me into your home. Isn't that enough without teaching Lance a lesson?" I asked in disbelief.

His gaze darkened into an unreadable hue. "Not even close. And we can talk about the whys another time. Now tell me. Did you contribute to the relationship?" he asked.

I nodded.

"You obviously don't have a bank account, so was yours joint?"

I glanced over at Central Park behind the gauzy curtains, unable to face him while I, again, managed a nod.

"And you're not the type to sit around and eat bonbons while your man works his fingers to the bone to provide for you."

I swallowed hard. "I used to work. But later in the relationship … I think I was brainwashed," I muttered, embarrassed.

He burst out laughing. "Considering the you I've known for less than twenty-four hours, I'd have to agree with you. What brought you out of the fog and into the light?"

I set my jaw. "I don't want to talk about that right now."

He studied me through narrowed eyes. "Eventually you will," he stated.

I blinked. "What kind of lesson?" I asked, changing the subject. "I mean, no blood or broken bones, right?"

He grinned. "No, I like my bones intact."

I rolled my eyes. "You know what I mean."

"I'll be utterly civilized. I can't promise Garrett will behave the same way, but he'll only act if provoked. Ex-Navy SEAL and all that."

"Who is Garrett?" I asked.

"Our bodyguard."

There it was again. That possessiveness in his words and tone. Just like *my* room, *our* bodyguard presumed we were in a relationship of some kind. We barely knew one another. What I did know was that he unequivocally turned me on in a way no man ever had. He also made me feel safe, wanted, and cared for.

But I was starting over, I reminded myself, and that included being smarter. What that entailed, I hadn't yet decided.

"All done with the questions?" he asked.

I managed to nod.

He hit one button. "Daltry? Gabriel Dare."

I ran my tongue over my dry lips. "You have him on autodial?" I asked loudly, then snapped my mouth shut as Gabe continued, his eyes on me as he spoke to Lance.

"I'm not so hot, and I'm not your buddy. Not anymore. Just giving you a heads-up. I'm cancelling all my accounts with you effective immediately. Just to be clear, do not make any more trades in my name. All my stocks and finances will be transferred by end of business today."

My eyes opened wide. I'd had no idea Lance managed Gabe's financial accounts. Then again, Lance was with the best-known firm in Manhattan, and Gabe clearly did business with only the best. Their relationship had just ended … because of me.

The blood drained from my head, and I sank deeper into the bed, lowering myself against the mattress that had given me such a good night's sleep. Now it supported me when I started to shake.

Gabe walked over and placed a firm hand on my shoulder. His touch burned my skin, reassuring me as well as confusing me.

"Not that I owe you an answer," Gabe said into

the phone, still speaking to Lance. "But if you want an explanation, I'm happy to provide one. Because you're a fucking prick who doesn't know how to treat a lady, that's why."

Gabe was defending me. Surprise, gratitude, and a host of unfamiliar emotions washed over me. My own parents hadn't defended me throughout my teenage years. Lance sure as hell had never truly supported me in any way. Yet Gabe was pulling what had to be million-dollar accounts from Lance's firm. *Because of me.*

I didn't know what to do with this. I didn't want to owe him, and yet gratitude flowed through my veins like freshly tapped maple syrup. Yeah, I remembered that day in elementary school. *Useless information*, I reminded myself and focused instead on the strength of Gabe's hand on my shoulder.

I started breathing again, picking up on Gabe's words mid-conversation. "I'm not answering any more of your damned questions about Izzy, and I don't expect she'll want to hear from you again."

I had never been called that before. I liked it.

Whatever Lance said, Gabe smirked and said, "I want her things delivered to my office immediately. Any money she came into your relationship with, I expect a check for that amount on my desk by the end of the week. And tack on interest."

Now I could still hear Lance shouting into the phone as Gabe disconnected the call and tossed the phone onto the bed.

"You okay?" he asked me.

I nodded. Then I did the dumbest thing I could do considering all the changes I'd promised myself I'd make in my life. I jumped up, flung my arms around his neck, and kissed him. Full on the lips. His masculine scent overwhelmed me, causing a fluttering deep in my belly and a quickening between my thighs. But his firm lips didn't move.

He didn't respond.

Didn't melt like I was melting.

Disappointment filled me, followed quickly by humiliation I was only too familiar with. How many times had I tried to seduce Lance, only to have him pull my arms off him so he could roll over, claiming exhaustion?

I'd overreacted, mistaking help for something more, and since I didn't need or want that *something* at this point in my life, I shored up my defenses and pulled away.

"Well. Now that I've properly thanked you, we can move on." I fought the blush I knew had formed on my cheeks.

"You're welcome," he said but didn't release me. He merely held on more tightly, his fingers digging into my wrists, pulling at my shoulders, all of which had the unfortunate effect of turning me on even more.

We stared into each other's eyes, and my breathing grew shallow. Oh hell, I was nearly panting with need, my breasts straining against the already-tight tank. I didn't understand this side effect of rejection.

But if he was rejecting me, why hadn't he let me go? "I don't understand." I could have been talking about his actions or mine.

"You will, Iz. In time."

I shivered at his shortening of my name. "How much time?"

A seductive smile tipped his lips, making it seem like he was far from disinterested. "I want to fuck you, kitten, but when I do, it won't be about gratitude. And it will be on my terms."

"Oh."

Lance never used the word *fuck* in bed, and if he had, it wouldn't have had me nearly coming from the sound alone.

My lips parted, and he swooped in, sliding his mouth over mine, all too briefly but enough for a taste.

A tease.

He yanked back harder on my wrists, and at the same time, he nipped at my lips. It stung there, while between my legs, a fullness the likes of which I'd never experienced before began to throb. Slick moisture dampened my underwear. Swaying forward, I moaned into his mouth.

At which point he released me. Only his strong arm around my waist prevented me from falling. My head spun from his seductive scent, his arousing kiss, the firm tone of his voice. Confusion and more warred inside me.

Gabe stepped back, apparently having none of the same problems. "I need to take care of some things at work. When I get back, we'll talk about your plans."

Plans. I blinked. That's right. I had plans. It was a good thing he was going to the office. Distance would do me some good and remind me I didn't need a man to make my life complete.

Nor did I need him to make me come. Something I planned to do as soon as Gabe left for the office.

* * *

Isabelle: The Secret Room

After I'd showered and taken care of… *things*, I headed into the kitchen to find Gabe had left me a note. "Iz"—there was that shortened name again, and I couldn't suppress a smile—"went to the office. Make yourself at home. And be good while I'm gone."

I didn't know how to be anything else.

I poured coffee from a pot Gabe had left for me, from a coffee maker built into the backsplash in the kitchen, and turned on the TV. The morning news droned around me as I toasted a bagel, slathered it with cream cheese, and settled in to eat. And to think.

At the moment, I was … for lack of a better word, stuck. At least with my money and clothes arriving, thanks to Gabe's demand, I'd feel more like myself, more in control of myself and my life. Then I could set about pondering what I wanted to do with my life.

The last time I'd been on my own and at a crossroads, I'd set out for New York City, to Parsons School of Design on a scholarship. It had led to an internship and, ultimately, a job after graduation at Lisa Stern Designs, a one-woman design firm that catered to various types of clientele, from home renovations to the occasional country club overhaul. I'd been hungry to learn, to work, but I'd also yearned for love and a relationship where I contributed and was a valued, equal partner.

That had been my one weakness, one Lance had homed in on. Before I knew it, I'd swapped a smart set of dreams for less practical ones he'd destroyed. And though I should be over that need, the yearning for family and the need to belong still lived inside me. However, I needed to be intelligent, and this time, I would be.

I sipped my coffee and sighed in pleasure at the perfect-tasting brew just as Gabe's home phone rang. One ring, and an answering machine picked up. Next thing I heard was an older woman's voice over the phone line.

"Good morning, Mr. Dare, this is Amelia. I won't be able to make it in to clean today, after all. I have a family emergency, but in all likelihood, I can get there tomorrow. I hope this doesn't cause you too much of an inconvenience. I'll have the spare room taken care of first thing in the morning. Only call me back if the timing doesn't work for you."

Cleaning. I wrinkled my nose. The apartment itself was pristine, as if it had been professionally sanitized just yesterday, so I couldn't imagine Gabe being upset his cleaning woman had cancelled. Then again, if he needed that spare room taken care of today, that was something I could do. Making myself useful around here would feel good, since I was already worried about taking advantage.

A quick search in the cabinets and pantry turned up cleaning supplies, but before I lugged everything into the spare room, the door to which had been closed yesterday, I figured I'd peek and see just what it needed.

I walked down the hallway, turned the knob, and

let myself in. The bed was unmade, the sheets rumpled, pillows dented and haphazardly strewn around. Who had slept in here? I stepped farther into the room, noting the furnishing was starker than Lucy's room, less warm and welcoming, the only furniture a king-sized four-poster bed, nightstands, and an armoire. No television. No clock or iPod holder. No pictures on the walls. I eased past the bed, which boasted black satin sheets and comforter, taking it all in.

I inhaled, and Gabe's cologne surrounded me. I looked into the bathroom, finding it, too, needed cleaning. There were towels on the floor, a toothbrush and open toothpaste on the vanity.

A glance down showed me everything I needed to know and wished I hadn't seen. Plastic condom wrappers in the garbage can.

My stomach heaved, and my heart stupidly squeezed in my chest. I didn't know how long I stood there staring, trying to make sense of this man I didn't know.

He'd made sure to keep me out of this room, and now I knew why. He'd had sex in this room. Recently. The evidence forced me to confront the ugly truth. No sooner had he rescued me from the police station than he'd decided to let Naomi go.

I'd known, of course, but I'd been too thrown by

the events of the night to process the cold, methodical reality. He'd had no problem dumping the woman he'd currently been involved with, the decision made in an instant. What did it say about his heart, or lack of one?

Having been on the receiving end of being cheated on, I didn't like knowing Gabe was essentially capable of the same thing. Or, if not cheating, so easily walking away from a relationship he was in.

I eased out of the room and headed for the other side of the apartment and paused in front of the master bedroom where Gabe slept. Yet he obviously *fucked* in the other room clear across the way. That was brutal.

I want to fuck you, kitten. But when I do, it won't be about gratitude. And it will be on my terms. I shivered, my knees nearly buckling at the memory of his seductive voice, the scent of his masculine, woodsy cologne, and his touch that ripped every one of my defenses to shreds. How easily I'd nearly succumbed.

Thank God that room had brought me back to reality, I thought, as panic set in. I needed air. Needed to breathe and think, clear of this apartment, where everything reminded me of the Gabe he'd shown me so far. How long before I saw the other side? The way I'd finally seen Lance's other side?

I patted my pockets, making sure I had my money

on me before hitting Lucy's room to grab my flip-flops, slide them onto my feet, and make my way out the door. As it slammed shut behind me, I realized I was now locked out of the apartment. I had no key to get back in until Gabe returned.

But did I want to go back? To the Gabe who I'd just learned was capable of cutting off his feelings so easily? Because for all that I told myself I didn't want another relationship, I knew better than to think I could stay here and eventually not surrender to Gabriel Dare.

Chapter Five

Isabelle: Lost in Time

I spent the day at the public library. Between the Internet and access to the *New York Times*, I began a job search. Although it had been awhile since I'd been employed, I did have a degree from Parsons and a previous employer who'd appreciated my work.

Although I'd definitely call Lisa, my old boss, on Monday, for now, the best I could do was make a list of impressive interior designers. I culled names I'd seen in magazines or had met through people in Lance's crowd, moving on to magazines and listings there. Finally, there was nothing more I could do until the workweek began.

I bought hotdogs from a street vendor for lunch, picked up a paperback at a nearby bookstore, and settled under a tree to read. Yeah, I know I was supposed to take some time and think, but I didn't like the way my thoughts were leading me, the yearning to go back to Gabe. How could I be so drawn to a man I didn't know? And why, oh why did I want to learn more? Getting lost in a book made more sense than racking my brain for answers I just didn't have.

By four p.m., my stomach was grumbling, I was tired and cranky, and after a day with a book, I'd come to the realization that there was no shame in not having figured out my life's plan after a mere twenty-four hours. It's not like I knew ahead of time I would be leaving my home for the unknown. At least now I was in a better position than if I'd woken up at a cheap motel with even less money in my pocket. And I decided I was through running away from my problems. Which meant I'd better head back and deal with the man who was causing the hodgepodge of feelings swirling in my gut.

I walked back to the sprawling apartment building and stopped by the doorman, who was not the same man who'd been on duty last night.

"Can I help you?" he asked.

"Is Mr. Dare in?"

"You must be Ms. Masters. He's been calling down every few minutes asking if you'd returned yet."

My eyes opened wide. It never dawned on me that Gabe would be concerned. It should have, but I was too thrown by … well, everything. I bit down on my lip. "Please call up and tell him I'm on my way?"

He smiled, treating me to a kindly look that made me think he was a father or a grandfather. Someone who also cared about people. Someone unlike my own parents. And on that unpleasant thought, I headed for the elevator, holding my breath, suddenly nervous.

The elevator doors opened, and I was stunned to find him waiting in the darkened, moody hallway, arm braced on the doorframe. He wore dark jeans and a long-sleeved, collared shirt, white, unbuttoned enough to tempt yet still give him that in-control, dangerously sexy air. His dark brown hair was tousled, as if he'd run his fingers through it in frustration more than a few times.

His eyes lit on me, and in that instant, longing caught in my throat, along with a healthy dose of wariness. Because no matter what I felt when I laid eyes on him, this morning's hard truths hadn't changed. And though I'd returned, I needed to understand what was going on between us before I could stay.

I stepped out and paused in front of him.

"You're okay." The words came out a mix of anger and relief.

I swallowed hard. "Yes."

"And how should I have known? You've been

gone since early this morning." He stepped forward then stopped himself, visibly holding himself back from me.

I winced. "I suppose I should have left you a note, but—"

"Yes, you should have."

I looked down, chastened, hating it and yet … oddly affected by his mix of emotions. Because that meant he still cared? Desired me?

Was that what *I* wanted?

I thrust my fingers into my tangled hair. "I'm sorry if you thought—"

"You have no idea what I was thinking." He gestured inside his apartment with a flick of his wrist.

Even as a part of me rebelled at his command, I strode past him, head high, acknowledging the part of me that was pleased he'd been concerned. When was the last time anyone had thought about my welfare?

He slammed the door shut behind him before turning back to face me. "Do you want to know what went through my mind?"

I swallowed hard. "Of course."

"Let's see. First, I thought Daltry had come by. I wondered if you'd changed your mind and left with him," Gabe bit out.

Oh, Gabe. "I wouldn't just pick up and leave after you've been so kind."

"I thought we'd gone over this. I'm not kind," he said in a tone meant to convince me.

He failed.

"Well, to me you are." And suddenly it didn't matter what he'd done to Naomi; *I* was different. He treated me better. Or was I deluding myself as I'd done with Lance? My stomach tumbled at the thought. "Do you want to know where I've been?" I asked.

"Go on."

I breathed out, elaborating on my day. "First I went to the public library so I could look through job listings and newspapers. I made lists and planned calls for Monday. Then I spent the day in the park. Reading. And thinking."

"By any chance, did that thinking include whether or not you should stay with me?"

I nodded.

He reached out and nabbed my hand, linking his big fingers through mine, tightening incrementally. His closeness eased some of the lingering tension, and my shoulders lowered as I allowed myself to relax beneath his touch. With a tug, he pulled me closer, invading my personal space, nuzzling his chin in my hair.

I closed my eyes and sighed, and when I breathed in, the expensive cologne I'd come to associate with him wrapped around me and lit me up from the inside out, like a firecracker with an ever-shortening fuse. I squeezed my thighs together to alleviate the ache that both excited and unnerved me at the same time.

"Don't leave." He turned me to face him.

My heart sped up in my chest. I should want to run, not wrap myself around him and never let go.

"I need you to say it." His grip on me tightened.

With his jaw clenched and his eyes imploring, I answered from the heart. "I won't." I tried not to panic at the commitment that statement implied and reassured myself that I'd find a job and make this new situation work. Whatever it meant for *us*, that would have to play itself out.

When stark relief etched his handsome face, I knew I'd pleased him, and a corresponding sense of peace settled inside of me, making me wonder—what *was* this unspoken thing between us? I didn't understand it.

I wanted more even as I fought against the sensations because they threatened me—more accurately, they threatened the sense of independence I'd told myself I needed.

Gabe slid his hand through my hair, tugging until I responded with a whimper. Okay, I clearly liked that dominating side of him. It was something I'd never experienced before but obviously responded to. Something else to think about later, I thought. Another facet of myself to explore when the opportunity arose.

"I'm going to kiss you now," he informed me. "And this has nothing to do with gratitude," he muttered and sealed his mouth over mine.

Holding me firmly, he slid his tongue over my lips once, twice, demanding entry. As if I'd deny him. Just the touch of his tongue set off fireworks inside me, and I responded to everything about the man. Everything he took, I wanted to give. Everything he provided, I craved more of. He must have understood because his tongue tangled with mine, tasting the far reaches of my mouth, sucking, pulling, learning every part of me, while I turned to liquid at each slip and glide, every thrust and parry.

This was being kissed. It was being told that I mattered. Even the way he sank his hand into my hair and held on let me know that, as much as he was dominating me, he *yearned* for me too. He needed the connection between us as badly as I did. The intensity was furious, fast and sudden, but I needed it, and somehow he sensed as much. My nipples puckered tight, beading until they were begging for Gabe's touch. His kiss held a direct line to my sex. But physical responses aside, the emotional yielding inside me explained so much more, screaming for me to believe that I could trust this man. A virtual stranger in so many ways, yet my body knew him already. Why else would worry flee from my mind, a foggy, blessed euphoria taking its place?

He broke the kiss but didn't release me, instead dragged his lips over my jaw and down to where my shoulder met my neck and slid his tongue over my skin. I trembled as he found an erogenous zone I hadn't realized I possessed. Cream coated my panties. Though I should be embarrassed at my easy acquiescence, it felt too good, desire melding into a whirlpool of burning need. A hard nip of my skin startled me into awareness, the sting of pain taking me by surprise, and I yelped out loud. Before I could struggle against him, a shock of ecstasy pulled me back into the vortex, reaching downward to my full, damp pussy.

Shaking, I crawled closer, finding his rock-hard erection behind a denim barrier, awaiting me. I needed him so badly. Could come so easily. I trembled and moaned. "Oh God."

"No, Iz. Just me." His breath was hot in my ear, and even his deep chuckle sent shooting sparks of awareness through me. "I want to fuck you right now. I want to slide into you when I'm completely bare. Feel your hot walls pulse around me until I come inside you and you feel everything I can give you."

Holy mother. Knees knocking, body shaking, only Gabe's hold on the back of my neck and the way he braced an arm around my waist kept me standing.

"Is that what you want, kitten?"

I moaned my assent. "Yes. Yes, take me now."

A masculine groan shuddered through him. "My bedroom," he muttered, his grip tightening.

That one word cleared my head enough for me to remember the other room in the house, the one with the rumpled sheets, the scent of sex, and the condoms in the trash that had sent me running.

"No. I can't."

Gabe lifted his head and stared into my eyes, disbelief flashing in the smoldering depths. He didn't ask for an explanation, but I heard the silent demand anyway.

"Not like this." I repeated his reason for not kissing me earlier, although his explanation for stopping was very different from mine now.

Again, he waited, as if he were entitled to an explanation but wouldn't demean himself to ask.

I swallowed over the lump lodged in the back of my throat. "I heard your housekeeper cancel on the answering machine and thought I could help you out by cleaning since she couldn't. She promised you she'd take care of the other room," I said in a rush. "The one with the closed door. So I … went in and saw … everything."

His eyes darkened in anger.

Because I'd crossed that threshold where I didn't

belong? Lance's triggers had been far less. "I wasn't snooping. I was trying to help."

"Fuck." He looked away.

His reaction hurt, and I braced myself for the lecture to come.

Without warning, his grip on me eased. I looked up to find him staring down at me, his gaze unexpectedly soft. "Don't ever be afraid of me, Isabelle. I'm not him." His calming voice soothed me.

I nodded and realized I was shaking, that fear had indeed taken me over. "Yelling was Lance's preferred form of communication. That or complete disdain followed by deafening silence." Which had left me feeling as bereft and as alone as I'd been as a child.

"Anything more?" he asked through gritted teeth.

"No," I assured him. "Lance knew how to wound without touching."

A muscle worked in his jaw. "My anger wasn't at you." He soothed me with caring strokes of his fingers over my throat and neck. "It was at myself. That there was anything in that room for you to find."

I shook my head. "I didn't exist to you then. But I'm coming off a long-term, bad relationship. So bad it would be a mistake to just jump into something now. We don't really know each other." I blushed, knowing how immature and naive I must sound, and yet I meant every word.

I might be moving in, allowing myself to rely on him based on an innate feeling of trust I had never felt for anyone before, not even Lance at his most gracious and charming. But sleeping with him was something else entirely.

He brushed my hair off my cheek, his touch warming me where I'd been cold. "I wouldn't cheat on you."

"But Naomi—"

"I didn't cheat on her either."

"No, you broke it off as if it meant nothing. As if she meant nothing." My teeth bit into my bottom lip. "And if you could do that to her, you could do it to me just as easily." When he got bored. Or realized I wasn't as interesting as he apparently found me now.

He ran a hand over his eyes. "If I tell you it's because she did mean nothing, you'll think I'm a cold bastard, but it's the truth." He shoved his hand into his pockets.

It didn't help, but at least he'd been honest. "Okay."

"No, not okay. But you have to understand something else." He tucked his hand beneath my chin, raising my eyes to his. "She's not you. Nobody's been you."

At his heartfelt words, my heart slammed against my chest. I didn't know what to say or how to feel. I only knew I liked the emotions he evoked in me way too much.

"Just know I wouldn't deliberately hurt you. And I'm. Not. Him."

I managed a nod. "That much I know." I did.

"So we're good?" he asked.

"Yes." But there was something else I needed to say, and it wouldn't come easily.

He narrowed his gaze. "I can tell there's a but. Just say it."

I managed a nod, swiping my tongue over my dry lips and reaching deep for courage. "Nobody's been there for me the way you have, and you barely know me, no matter what crazy attraction exists between us."

"I know you, Iz."

A shudder rippled through me. I forced myself to continue. "And today, I took off because I didn't like the way that room made me feel. I needed air, and I didn't realize I was locked out until the door shut behind me. But I didn't stay away to teach you a lesson or act like a jealous brat. It never dawned on me that you'd be worried." I blinked and glanced away. "My parents never were. Lance never was. Your caring and protectiveness, it's new to me."

Understanding and something more turned his expression warm and soft. "It's new to me too," he admitted. "You're my kitten," he said, his voice gruff.

Unsure of how to interpret that, I tilted my head, looking up at him.

A knowing smile lifted his mouth into a disarming, sexy grin. "You're brave one minute, skittish the next. You need to be gentled, to learn that the hand that's stroking you can be trusted."

As he spoke, his thumb glided over my neck, pausing at my rapidly beating pulse. "I can't change what or who came before you, but I can tell you that you're different. For me, to me. I don't understand why, I just *know*. And if you give me the chance, I'll prove it." He continued to glide his thumb back and forth against my skin, gentling me, as he'd said.

My eyes fluttered closed. "I've never had anyone in my life I could truly trust." The people I was supposed to trust betrayed me, and the one I'd chosen had done the same.

"Well, now you do." His hand traveled upward, until he brushed my jaw, then my lips, with his thumb.

Darned if I didn't fall right back into that soft, easy spot he'd taken me to before. Feeling brave, I licked, then nipped at his finger.

He groaned and smoothed my own moisture over my lips. "Give me a chance," he said in a gruff voice that made me tingle.

My stomach chose that moment to emit an unattractive growl. I just knew my cheeks turned red.

Gabe merely chuckled. "My kitten needs food."

I forced my heavy eyelids open, embarrassed at the sound. "I haven't eaten since a hotdog I bought for lunch."

His frown told me what he thought of that. "Come. I'll feed you."

Which brought up my other concern that was equally if not more dangerous to my peace of mind. He wanted to feed me, he'd said. I could feed myself, by why argue? He spoke how he spoke, and I responded to it. But I couldn't help wondering just how I could reinvent myself if I jumped right into another man's home, not to mention his bed.

Although Gabe didn't seem like just any other man. He already felt important to me, something I didn't, couldn't comprehend. So maybe the key lay in getting to know him better and, as a result, learning more about myself and why I responded to him so strongly.

But I wondered how long I could hold out against his seductive charm.

Chapter Six

Gabe: Staking a Claim

Gabe couldn't explain the primitive need to take care of Isabelle, to convince her that here, she could heal and find everything else she needed in life. With him. It wasn't taking in a stray, as his brother had accused, it was caring for a woman he was completely drawn to and always had been. One he sensed would upend everything he'd told himself he wanted out of life post-Krissie, his deceased wife. Although he'd told himself he would never open himself up again, being given a chance with Isabelle made him change his mind. Now he had to change hers.

But first, he could focus on something as simple as dinner. His housekeeper left him with enough home-cooked meals that he had his choice, but tonight he wanted to cook more than frozen and microwaved food.

While Izzy showered, Gabe pulled out two steaks from the freezer, defrosted them, and soon had them cooking on his Thermador indoor grill. Lucy had insisted his kitchen be decorated with only the best, and over time, he'd come to appreciate cooking for himself once in awhile. Looking after Isabelle was a pleasure he'd never thought he'd have.

He microwaved baking potatoes and set the table for two, even impressing himself with his speed. She seemed to take her time in the shower, and he hoped she was relaxing and not working herself into a panicked, frenzied need to leave.

He'd just pulled the steaks from the grill when the doorbell rang, surprising him. He answered it, not at all happy to find his brother on the other side.

Decklan stepped inside without Gabe's invitation, took a deep inhale, and grinned. "Smells like I'm just in time for supper."

"The hell you are. You're leaving."

His brother shot him a knowing look. "That answers question number one. She's still here."

Gabe nodded. "Yes, she is, and I intend for her to remain. So leave before you scare her away. She's not too fond of you, as I recall."

Decklan shook his head. "That's why I come bearing gifts." He held up a plain brown bag branded with the local pharmacy on the front.

"Gabe?" Izzy's voice called to him from the bedrooms.

"Be right there!" Gabe turned back to his brother. "I don't know what you've got in that bag, but take it and go home." He wanted Izzy to himself over dinner. Time to explore her past, present, likes, and dislikes and to let her get to know him.

Before Decklan could answer, Gabe became aware of a soft, feminine scent.

"I didn't know you were expecting company." Isabelle joined them, wearing another of Lucy's outfits, sweats that were again snug, emphasizing every inch of her delectable—*not model-thin, thank God*—body. She glanced at Decklan, her eyes opening in surprise. "Oh. It's you."

"Don't sound so happy to see me," his brother said, his tone filled with more amusement than when he'd been dealing with her last night.

"You were rude to me," she informed him in a haughty tone, nose in the air.

Gabe barked out a laugh.

"You were under arrest!" Decklan shot back.

"Bogus charges." She folded her arms across her chest and glared.

Gabe looked at his brother and grinned. "Guess she doesn't want you here any more than I do right now."

Decklan didn't seem bothered. "Not even if I have something for you?" Focused on Isabelle, he held up the bag.

Now he had Gabe wondering what the hell was in it that had his always-serious brother sounding so proud of himself.

Isabelle cocked an eyebrow and stepped forward. Gabe's gaze fell to her bare feet and hot pink toenails. Damn, he'd like to suck each one slowly, nibbling, and listen to her moan as he worked his way upward—

"Let me see." Her voice broke Gabe's daydream.

Decklan handed her the bag, and Isabelle snatched it away, peering inside. Her eyes widened, and she stared at him, open-mouthed. "You… I… This is actually *thoughtful*!"

Gabe was torn between laughing at the notion that she didn't think his brother had thoughtful in him and jealous that she now stared at Decklan with a new-found respect.

"Thank you, Ms. Masters. Don't I get at least a peck on the cheek for the effort?" he asked.

A pink blush stole up Izzy's cheeks. Gabe wanted to be the only one responsible for putting that flush on her face.

She stepped forward, and Gabe growled. Literally

growled. "Go home, Decklan. Izzy and I have plans."

"Don't be rude! He came all the way over here to give me—"

Gabe grabbed the bag and looked inside. "Tums? He gave you Tums, and you're gushing all over him?"

Decklan burst out laughing while Izzy stood between them, obviously confused at Gabe's possessive behavior. Gabe didn't understand it either. He only knew that until he and Izzy had something solid, no other man was getting between them. His brother and his dime-store gifts included.

"I actually have to be going. I have a date," Decklan said, clearly holding back his amusement. "I just figured, based on my brother's behavior last night, he wanted to keep you, and I'd best bring by a peace offering." He shrugged. "Considering what I just witnessed, nothing's changed, so I'll be seeing you around here, Isabelle. Assuming he doesn't drive you away with his jealousy first."

"Go home," Gabe muttered, embarrassed at being caught acting like an ass by the only man in this world he could actually trust around his woman.

Decklan turned to go. Gabe figured he'd make things right with his sibling tomorrow.

"Wait," Izzy said, stopping Decklan's retreat.

His brother glanced back at her.

"Peace offering accepted," she said with a grateful smile on her beautiful face, leaving Gabe with the thought that if a bottle of Tums turned her into a beaming angel, he couldn't wait to bestow more intimate, unexpected presents on his favorite girl.

Chapter Seven

Isabelle: Clarity

I was ravenous and devoured the most delicious steak, well aware of Gabe's eyes on me the whole time. We sat in a small breakfast nook in the kitchen, eating on a white and beige granite tabletop. Gabe pulled his seat close to mine, and though I should've been uncomfortable, I wasn't because I was too amused by what had gone down between Gabe and Decklan over me.

Me.

"What's so funny?" Gabe asked me, wiping his mouth with a napkin before placing it back in his lap.

"I can't say I've ever been the object of a pissing contest before."

He leaned on one arm. "Can't say I've engaged in one before either."

I had a difficult time believing him. "No big blocks

of real estate you've wanted? No club takeovers?"

"I was talking about women." He paused. "You saw the bedroom."

No need for me to ask which one.

He rubbed a hand over his stubbled jaw, obviously considering what to say next, and a gnawing ache ate at my stomach as I waited for him to continue.

"That room has been the extent of my dealings with women for more years than I can remember." He steepled his fingers and stared at me for a long while before finally speaking. "I normally don't bring women to my bed, but I don't want to be in their space either."

"Too intimate?" I asked him, leaning back in my seat, as if I had no problem with his women or his habits.

"Much." Those dark eyes probed into mine.

"That's sad," I said, rising to my feet. I picked up my dish, then his, intending to clean up the meal.

He clamped his hand on my wrist. "Leave it."

"You cooked, I'll clean."

He didn't release me, his grip tightening. "It can wait. Amelia will be in tomorrow."

I shook my head in automatic denial. "I don't want to make extra work for her. I can—"

"But you won't." His voice brooked no argument.

I shook my hand free. "Mind if I ask why not?"

"I work too hard to make the life of those I care about easy, and I pay those who work for me too much for you to worry about it."

"Oh." I tried to see his point of view, but I'd grown up in an average house, where I was expected to take care of chores and help with daily tasks.

Even Lance, who brought in help for parties and had a cleaning service in weekly, had expected me to handle the everyday duties of running a house. But that wasn't the only thing about Gabe's proclamation that stood out. *I work too hard to make the life of those I care about easy.* I could understand him feeling that way about himself. His sister when she stayed over. Even his brother, when they weren't bickering.

But me? How had I become one of those he cared about in such a short span of time? *Don't you care about him?* a small voice in the back of my head asked.

I wanted to concentrate on understanding him. "Let me get this straight. You don't bring women into your bed. You don't go to their homes, hence the extra bedroom."

He inclined his head in agreement but remained silent, giving me a chance to formulate my next question, which I knew he wouldn't like, but I intended to ask it anyway.

"You've made it clear you want to … fuck me…"

Gabe's irises darkened to a stormy hue. "I do

want—and plan—to fuck you."

I'd chosen to repeat his word, a term I'd never used before.

At least not in a context relating to me and any man I'd ever been intimate with. Not that there'd been many. And I didn't appreciate the fact that my body didn't seem to care whether I used the word *fuck*, *sex*, or *making love*—all of those terms, when spoken in reference to myself and Gabe, turned my insides to mush and dampened the tiny g-string panties I'd been forced to borrow from the drawer in the bedroom.

"Your point, kitten?" His lean, chiseled body shook with barely leashed power and the restraint it took for him not to touch me.

I could see it. Feel it. I wanted him too, but I needed clarity more.

I rocked on my bare feet. "My point being, I'm in the room next to yours… Is that because the *other* room hasn't been cleaned?" I wrinkled my nose, unable to control the disdain in my tone.

He clenched his jaw tight, and his gaze slid away.

Right. I wrapped my arms around myself.

"It's not like I thought it out. And it's not like I had to since there was only that one room available."

I nodded. "Okay." It made sense. Hurt on some stupid level, but made sense.

He clenched his jaw. "Are you finished?" he asked,

clearly unhappy with the direction of my thoughts.

I shook my head. No, I was not finished, and he was about to get more upset because I had questions that demanded answers. He'd told me Naomi didn't mean much to him, but that could have been something he'd said to appease me.

I cleared my throat and forged ahead. "Was Naomi ever one of those people you care about, and whose life you wanted to make easy?" Before she'd stopped and he'd tossed her away.

Had he selected her, and those before me, used them, made their lives easy, and disposed of them when he was finished? When someone new and more appealing came along? Like Lance had done with me, except he hadn't had the decency to end things before starting up with someone else.

I figured I should at least know who and what kind of man Gabriel Dare really was.

You already know.

I ignored the voice in my head, the one filled with hopes and dreams that never came true but caused much damage in the pursuit.

Gabe lifted my chin, a favorite habit of his, forcing me to meet his gaze. To look into his handsome face, both rugged and chiseled to perfection at the same time.

"I told you before, and I'll say it again, clearer this

time. Naomi provided an outlet. Other women provided me with the same thing. A release and nothing more. And that's the last time I want to hear you put yourself in the same category as any one of them ever again."

My knees nearly buckled in relief, and how ridiculous was that? This man affected me on such a deep level that my emotions, which I'd promised to tuck safely away, were already engaged. It made no sense. And it frightened me beyond reason.

So I kept pushing, hoping with answers would come clarity. "But there was someone once. Another woman. A stray that your brother mentioned."

A muscle ticked in his cheek. "I'm a man of few words, and you've exhausted those tonight." His hand slid from my chin to cup my jaw. "I will say it's in the past."

"Good enough."

A smile teased his mouth.

"For now," I added, lest he think I gave up easily.

A low growl emanated from inside him. Next thing I knew, he lifted me into his arms and carried me out of the kitchen, through the entryway, and toward the two bedrooms in the back of the apartment.

"Gabe, wait!"

He paused at the end of the long hall. "This is the only time you get a choice," he said, his voice gruff.

My answer depended on which door he carried me through, but I couldn't give voice to the question, which would only reveal a need for more than sex, one that, though I'd alluded to it, I didn't want him to see so blatantly on display.

"Time's up," he said and kicked open *his* bedroom door.

*   *   *

Isabelle: Behind the Chosen Door

Gabe slid me down the length of his body, and I responded with liquid heat to every hard inch I touched.

A soft moan reverberated around us, and I was shocked to realize it had come from me.

"Clothes off," Gabe said, sounding like a man very much in control.

My eyes opened wide at the command.

I was curvier than the women he dated, had compared myself more than once at the country club, yet I followed his instruction to the letter, pulling on the drawstring, releasing the sweatpants so they pooled at my feet. I shook them off. Tee shirt came next, up, over my head, and onto the floor.

His stormy gaze never wavered, merely darkened as I stood before him in that tiny thong and my one and only bra. At least it was lace, I thought, trying hard not to duck my head in mortification, my hands itching to cover myself. Somehow I knew he wouldn't allow it, and I kept my arms at my sides.

"Everything, Iz." He folded his arms across his broad chest.

I noted *he* was still dressed, yet again, I did as he commanded, never once thinking not to listen. Warning bells sounded in the back of my brain, a place that should have been front and center but was somehow very far away.

The panties, I slipped off quickly. The bra, that wasn't so easy. I'd always been self-conscious of my breasts, too big for the rest of my body, except my generous hips and ass, another sore subject for me. Over time, Lance hadn't been complimentary, and it was only now that I understood why. By making me feel like nobody else would want me, he'd kept me with him far longer than I should have been.

Braver now, my hands went for the back hook on my bra, releasing the clasp and letting the garment fall to the floor.

"Eyes open." His voice sounded like a clap of thunder, sharp and booming.

I hadn't realized I'd closed them and forced myself

to meet his gaze. Approval and heat—so much heat—lit up his handsome face. There was no doubt that this man wanted me. Every rounded, curvy inch. Liquid trickled from my thighs, and I had no doubt he noticed. He had to, and I wanted to die of embarrassment that his orders were making me this hot. Wet. So needy I wanted to rub myself against him like the kitten he called me.

"Good girl."

The compliment rippled through me, cultivating a deeper yearning, more moisture.

He walked over, and the powerful scent of his cologne enveloped me like a safety net. I desperately longed for his touch but didn't know how to ask.

He reached out and cupped my shoulder in a firm grip, and just like that, I settled. My muscles relaxed, and my head felt less heavy. A pleased smile curved his lips, telling me somehow he'd known what I needed and was happy I'd responded.

Confused and so very aroused, I blew out a long stream of air … and waited. For what, I didn't know, but he seemed to be moving at his own pace, and I was content to allow him the privilege.

"You're perfect," he said, tipping his head down for a sweet kiss on my lips.

Sweet?

Yes, I thought, contradictorily sweet, and I arched

up on my tiptoes for more.

He abruptly broke contact. "On the bed."

I forced my heavy eyelids open and scrambled to do as he said. Never even questioned it.

"Back against the pillows, legs open, hands on the headboard."

I narrowed my eyes.

A muscle ticked on one side of his jaw. "Trust me to give you what you need."

I should've hesitated.

I told myself to take back some control.

Instead, I complied.

I scooted my butt backward and leaned against the pillows. Spreading my legs wide? Not so easy. I parted my thighs, feeling open and exposed. Silly. I focused on my other task, raising my hands to the slats on the headboard—until I realized the effect it had of thrusting my breasts out for his view. Well, that took my mind off my lower half, and I dropped my elbows to lessen the feeling of being so exposed.

The loud clap of Gabe's hands startled me. "Eyes," he ordered, pointing to his own. "On me always. Legs wider."

I managed a deep breath and exposed my wet self to his hot stare.

"And relax those arms, kitten, or you'll be sore for no reason," he said, his tone gentling as he stepped closer to the bed and eased himself beside me.

He clasped one hand at the top of my thigh. "So fucking perfect," he murmured, and my heart swelled at the words.

Leaning in, he eased his lips over mine in a way I sensed meant he wouldn't be parting from me anytime soon. He slid that beautiful mouth back and forth over mine, moisture we created together causing a delicious slip and glide between us. His hand slid higher up my leg, inch by inch, until his thumb began a steady sweep over my bare mound, a place so long denied a gentle, caring touch.

I moaned again. This time I didn't care, arching my hips, seeking harder contact, more pressure. A light slap on my bare pussy startled me.

"One, eyes on me," Gabe said. "And two, I'll give you what you need. You only need to trust me to know what … and when."

"But—"

Another slap, this one slightly harder, the sting deeper. "Oh!" I gasped in outraged surprise only to be startled when the sting wore off and a pulsating warmth took its place. "Oohh," I whispered in sudden understanding as arousal replaced confusion.

My hips twisted against his hand, and I immediately caught myself, stopping the movement, no matter how badly I wanted the contact and pressure his palm could provide.

"Now you're getting the point," he said, pleased. Leaning close, he settled his stubbled face against my cheek, and I breathed him in, taking the scent that was Gabe into my bones.

"Let me make you feel good."

"Yes." The word came without thought.

He was still dressed, and I didn't care, my only thought centered on relief from the ache he'd caused and continued to stoke.

He lay between my legs and dipped his head, his warm breath flowing over the apex of my thighs. I wanted to arch up but didn't dare.

Trust me, he'd said.

Nobody had taken care of me. Everyone else's needs always came prior to my own. But this man seemed wholly focused on me and my needs, I thought, as his tongue slid over me and a long shudder shook through me. He licked and stroked, first one outer lip, then the other, teasing me with circular laps of his tongue, surrounding the one spot that begged for attention.

I gripped the headboard harder, holding on tightly, while he devoured every inch of me. Never had anyone lingered so long or groaned in such primal satisfaction at a job well done. He nibbled with his teeth, took long sweeps with his tongue, alternating them quickly and mercilessly until sensations collided, fighting for dominance. I climbed higher and higher still, his devoted attention to his task perfect, no place, no detail left out. My hips shook, and waves attacked me, rising but never peaking as Gabe kept me hanging, my climax so close yet just out of reach.

I was soaked with my own juices and from him, and I didn't care. He let out a low groan, and the vibrations skyrocketed through me, my sighs, moans, *oh Gods* echoing throughout the room. Stars flickered behind my eyes, and I was certain this was it, I was so ready to detonate, and the bastard eased off, changed pace, pulling me back down only to start all over again. Nobody had ever played me so thoroughly or so well.

Without warning, he thrust not one finger but two inside me at the exact moment he latched on to my clit with his teeth. I screamed. He curved his fingers, somehow finding an elusive spot that brought me to exquisite heights, shattering me into pieces that scattered into the air. I lost track of time and place, wholly and utterly spent.

I don't know how long a time passed, only that I came to myself slowly, my breathing catching up with my mind, my mind with my body, until I was able to focus. Somehow I was wrapped in Gabe's strong arms.

I reached for him, finding his shirt and not his skin. "You're still dressed," I said, disappointed. I wanted to see his body, the muscles I'd only imagined, the hot skin beneath the clothes. But I hadn't been given the pleasure of the view. I hadn't felt him in my hands, nor had I experienced him inside my body.

"I didn't want to rush things." He stared down at me, his expression more shuttered than before.

My heart beat a rapid staccato, fear replacing contentment. I struggled to sit, to pull away. If he didn't want me, what had that been about? Exposing me that way?

"Relax." His arms tightened, easing me back into him.

I shook my head, rebelling against his control. "I don't like these kind of games." Sex games? Games for pleasure? I wouldn't have thought I'd enjoy those, but he'd made me see that I could. But emotional games were something else, and he'd clearly pulled away, encasing himself in some sort of icy shell. This after making me melt all over him. That was just cruel.

Tears filled my eyes, and mortification rushed through me. "Let me go."

"I want you," he said, the words stilling my movements. "Maybe too much."

That caused a pain in my chest. "Explain."

His long silence frightened me, but since he wasn't releasing his tight hold, I had no choice but to wait out his explanation.

"I never have unprotected sex."

I wrinkled my nose. "I should hope not." Understanding dawned. "You don't have condoms?" Had he used them all up with—I quickly cut off that train of thought.

He groaned, his hand stroking my hair. "I have them."

"Then I really don't understand."

"Neither do I," he muttered, almost too low for me to hear.

I didn't get what was going on with him—a change of mind? Or not?

Uncomfortable being the only one undressed and vulnerable, I forced myself out of his embrace. "Explain or I walk," I said, jumping out of bed and searching for my clothes.

"Stop," he commanded in *that* voice.

Until he provided me with understanding that made sense, I wasn't falling under his spell again. Without worrying about the panties, I continued my jerky movements, pulling up the sweats and yanking the tee shirt over my head.

"I don't want anything between us when I come inside you," he finally said, the admission drawn from somewhere deep. "Skin to skin. Flesh to flesh. No barrier. I couldn't stand it."

I stilled. His words were soft, not spoken in that

take-charge way, yet my body responded, returning to the place where I ceded control willingly, without thought.

This was bad, I realized. Scary bad, this sudden deep, emotional need and connection between us. But it existed.

I looked up, met his gaze. He stared back, but his expression still held blank pieces, and my stomach churned uncomfortably.

He held out his hand.

I strode over, placing my palm in his. Decision made, nerves be damned. Whatever this was, we were in it together. Because what I'd found with Gabe behind his bedroom door was too strong to be denied.

I sensed there was more to why he hadn't … fucked me … than wanting us skin to skin. I shivered at the sensual prospect because I wanted it too. But it scared me. Badly.

I wondered what it would take for him to admit that it had scared him too.

Chapter Eight

Gabe: Coming to Terms

Shit, shit, shit.

Gabe swept the papers off his desk, sending everything flying onto the floor. He wasn't supposed to feel this way about anyone. Not ever again.

Ghosts flashed in front of his eyes, of those he'd loved and lost, and the one he hadn't really loved and should never have married. Now he had a woman in his bedroom asleep, and despite all his damned commands, she held all the power.

He'd learned about power exchange in order to feel in control—of himself and his life? And he had.

Until Isabelle.

He should have heeded his brother and not taken her home, but he'd listened to her sassy retorts, he'd looked into her eyes, and he'd been trapped. So here he was, sporting a hard-on the likes of which he'd never experienced, relief a couple of feet away, and he was doing something he'd never done before—depriving himself of what he wanted.

Because what he wanted was more than her body. He wanted her soul. And she was clearly nowhere near ready to give it to him.

His phone rang, and he answered without checking the caller ID. "Yeah."

"Good morning to you too, big brother."

"Lucy, what are you doing calling so early on the weekend?" If it was nine a.m. in New York, it was six a.m. in California.

"My other brother called and said you'd lost your mind over a woman, so I'm calling for information."

Gabe rolled his eyes. "I haven't lost my mind, Luce. Decklan exaggerates."

"Did you or did you not move her into my room?"

"So that's why you're calling. You're pissed you're being displaced."

Lucy burst out laughing. "I could care less about that. And I'll take that answer as a yes." She let out a whoop of joy.

"Tone it down," he muttered.

"Don't go all bossy on me. I'm flying home to meet her."

Gabe shook his head. "You'll do no such thing."

At least, not until he figured out what he was going to do with her.

"I was coming anyway. There's an island resort off the coast of Florida. It's called Eden. How cool is that? You can only go there via invitation. It's secluded, secretive, and exclusive, and we have the opportunity to open a nightclub there. I need to fill you in."

"Sounds intriguing," he said, meaning it.

"Oh, it is. Don't worry. I'll tell you all about it when I see you. And don't worry, I'll either stay with Decklan or get a room at one of our hotels."

He'd normally argue, but he didn't want anyone intruding on his time with Isabelle. "Thanks," he said to his sister.

"Anytime."

"You okay?" he asked her.

Lucy let out an exasperated breath. "Always. You don't need to worry about me." Her standard answer.

He set his jaw. "I raised you—"

"Hardly! I was sixteen when Mom and Dad died."

He swallowed hard. "Okay, then I got you through those horrid teenage years, with boys, dating, parties. You know, the hard shit."

"Oh yeah, you had to talk to me about sex and birth control."

"Someone did. Decklan sure as hell didn't want to

do it."

She giggled, sounding like she had that day. He'd cornered her by driving onto a highway and staying there until the painful talk ended.

"I remember. And that means I owe you," she said, her voice taking on a deeper, more serious tone. "So if you met a woman, I need to meet her too. Make sure she's good enough for you."

His heart swelled. Lucy and Deck were the only people he still let himself love. Of course, they were family. Gabe had to love them.

Then there was Isabelle.

Chapter Nine

Isabelle: Day of Reckoning

I woke up alone in Gabe's bed, conflicting emotions assailing me. On the one hand, I congratulated myself. I hadn't had sex with Gabe. On the other, he hadn't fucked me after proclaiming how much he wanted to … and if he'd wanted to, I wouldn't have said no.

I placated myself with the fact that last night I'd demanded and received answers to many if not all things pertaining to Gabe. I hadn't been a man's pushover this time. Score one for me. On the other hand, Gabe had commanded me to strip, told me to spread my legs open wide, and proceeded to slap me *there*. I'd not only allowed it, I'd come hard from the sensations. My cheeks burned, not just at the recollection but from the tingling between my thighs and the slick wetness there now.

And finally, this enigmatic man, who claimed he never brought women to his room and always used a condom, said he did not want to use one with me. He couldn't bear to have anything between us. Yet we hadn't had sex, and I hadn't seen him naked.

And I was in his bed this morning, all alone.

I shivered, my chills having less to do with the room temperature and everything to do with my current, naked state. As I slid from beneath the covers, I spotted a large tee shirt draped over a chaise lounge in the corner of the room. I shrugged and quickly covered myself.

Feeling more comfortable, I retrieved my panties from the floor and pulled them on before scooping up the rest of my clothing and heading for the door. I peeked out, then tiptoed across the hall, grateful I didn't run into Gabe or his housekeeper on the way. A shower and clothing would go a long way toward providing me with armor to face the day, not to mention the man himself.

An hour later, clean, blow-dried, dressed, and wearing makeup I'd borrowed from his sister, I braced myself and headed for the kitchen, only to find myself still alone.

When the telephone rang, I jumped, the sound startling me before I realized it wasn't the phone but the intercom for the doorman downstairs. I didn't plan to answer, but the ringing was insistent, and I finally caved, lifting the receiver. "Hello?"

"Ms. Masters?"

I wrinkled my nose. Either the doorman remembered me or Gabe had informed him I was staying here. "Yes?"

"There's a gentleman down here with suitcases he says are for you."

Lance? I wondered, my heart thudding inside my chest. Gabe had insisted he send over my things. I needed them desperately if I didn't want to spend the little money I had. If Lance had brought the check Gabe demanded, even better. But Gabe wasn't here as backup, and I had to wonder if Lance really would cave so easily.

It didn't matter, I decided. I couldn't rely on Gabe, or any one else, to deal with my ex for me. No more running, I reminded myself. I'd face him.

"Send him up, please." I hung up and smoothed my shaking hand over my wild hair.

A loud knock sounded on the door.

I entered the hall and faced the man I'd walked out on. His blond hair was slicked back, his blue eyes like ice and very cold. He'd dressed for the occasion in navy slacks and a button-down dress shirt, and his gaze raked over my sweats and tee shirt, a disgusted frown on the face I'd once considered handsome. That was before I had Gabe's dark visage as a counterpoint.

He stared without commenting.

I gripped the doorframe. "Where are my bags?" I looked beyond him but didn't see a cart or luggage behind Lance or in his hand.

"Did you really think I'd roll over just because the man you're currently whoring yourself for ordered me to?"

I narrowed my gaze. I should have known this wouldn't go smoothly. Should have suggested he leave my things downstairs. "No bags? Then I have nothing to say."

I started to close the door, but he braced his arm, blocking my ability to shut him out. "You don't know who you're dealing with."

I raised an eyebrow at that. "Of course I do. You're a cheating dirtbag who didn't know a good thing when he had it. Now, I suggest you leave before—"

"Before what? Your new boyfriend throws me out? He's not here, or do you really think I'm stupid enough to show up when he's home?"

"How would you know?"

"Money buys information. But you wouldn't know because you don't have any." He shook his head, making a tsking noise as he did so. "You're too naïve for your own good. A man like Gabe will grow bored of you soon enough. God knows I did."

I didn't care how many nerves he pricked, I refused to let him see how badly his words hurt me. I deliberately yawned, wanting to look bored.

Unfortunately, Lance appeared to be enjoying himself. He leaned in closer. "I only kept you around out of pity, you know. That and you kept a nice, clean house and did what I asked with little fuss. Not to mention, you were frigid enough that you didn't even know how often I took my pleasure elsewhere."

A red haze of fury erupted inside me, anger not just at how callously he treated me but how stupid I'd been for falling for him at all, believing his lies, and sticking around even once I knew better.

"If I was frigid, it was only because you didn't know what the hell you were doing, you lying, cheating son of a bitch." I gripped the frame so hard I was surprised I didn't break one of my fingers.

"Don't pull the righteous routine on me. How long was this going on behind my back?"

I didn't answer. He wouldn't believe me anyway.

"Gabriel Dare might be attracted to you. I was too, for a time. He'll grow bored just like I did. I only came here to let you know you won't be seeing one cent from me. You've taken enough."

Once again, he'd managed to find the best way to hurt me. My ears rang with all the insults he'd hurled, but I wouldn't let him break me. "You stupid, arrogant ass. I'd rather live on the streets than take anything from you."

"That can be arranged." A mean smile took hold, making me wonder how he'd kept this nasty part of himself hidden from me for so long.

I turned my back on him, and he grabbed my shoulder.

Touching me was the last straw. I spun around and kicked out, my bare foot landing in his groin.

"You bitch." He slapped me hard at the exact moment the elevator doors opened and Gabe stormed through in time to see Lance's hand make contact with my cheek.

Gabe's gaze swung from Lance to me before he hauled Lance up by his shirt, shoving his back against the wall, his fist connecting with the other man's jaw. "You don't hit women. But you especially don't hit this one," Gabe bit out, still holding Lance against the wall.

Lance glared but held his ground, not blinking.

"I specifically told you to bring her things to my office. Show up here again and you won't be able to walk out of here on your own."

"He almost didn't," I muttered. Between my kick and Gabe's punch, Lance appeared dazed and stunned.

And if I'd had on real shoes, that kick might have

done some damage. As it was, I worked my aching jaw back and forth.

Gabe released his hold, and Lance scrambled not to fall. He righted himself, straightening his shirt, throwing a glare Gabe's way. "This isn't over."

"If you mean you still owe her, you're right." Gabe stepped beside me, pulling me into him. I allowed the show of possession, knowing it would infuriate my ex.

Lance's scowl told me I was right. "She's not worth the trouble I promise you I can—and will—rain down on you," he said to Gabe, his words a clear threat.

Gabe's low snarl frightened even me. "That just shows how incredibly stupid, not to mention ignorant, you are."

I trembled and wrapped my arms around myself, silently admitting Lance was probably right. I wasn't worth the hassle, something Gabe might have just figured out—but at least he presented a united front to my ex.

Giving my shoulder a reassuring squeeze, Gabe strode into the darkened hallway and hit the down button for the elevator before turning to Lance. "I suggest you leave before I call the police. You're trespassing."

Lance wisely remained silent until he stepped into the open elevator. "Don't be a fool over a piece of ass," he called out to Gabe, timing his shout to coincide with the closing door.

* * *

Isabelle: Should I Stay or Should I Go?

Gabe watched the doors shut completely before turning his focus to me. Gaze narrowed, his stare came to rest on my cheek.

"I should have killed him when I had the chance."

He grabbed my hand and pulled me into the apartment, slamming the door shut behind me. Once in the kitchen, he stopped at the freezer and filled a Ziploc bag with ice.

"Wait here." He stormed off, returning with a white tee shirt. He wrapped the ice inside it and held the soft cotton against my face.

I winced.

"Sorry, but keep it there." He led me to the sofa in the living room and settled in beside me. "Are you okay?" He brushed my wayward curls off my shoulder.

I didn't want to enjoy his gentle ministrations as much as I did, and the words I had to say lodged in my throat before I managed to force them out.

"I'm leaving. You did a nice thing by letting me

stay, and we got carried away… Let me just say thank you and leave it at that." I placed the ice on the table.

He frowned and immediately held it back to my face. "Why did you let that bastard upstairs?" he asked, ignoring my statement.

Not that I was surprised. I decided to answer his questions first. "The doorman called. He said a man was downstairs with suitcases for me. I figured Lance would bring up my things, have his say, and go."

Gabe's eyes narrowed, raw anger lacing his features. "The *doorman* said he had luggage for you?"

I nodded.

"And he lied," Gabe said, his expression dark.

I nodded again. "When I asked how Lance knew you wouldn't be home, he mentioned something about money buying information."

Gabe shook his head in frustration. "I should have been one step ahead of him. It won't happen again," he promised.

I knew that, because I wouldn't be here. If Lance promised trouble, he meant it. Gabe didn't need aggravation in his life brought on solely because of me. That was just another reason for me to leave. My self-respect and need for independence were two more. Seeing Lance again only reinforced why I'd left him in the first place. I'd let Gabe's persuasive powers lure me into a sense of security that could only be another trap.

I grasped his wrist, pulling the ice away from my frozen skin. "It's cold."

He put the wrapped ice on the table. Bracing his hands on his knees, he appeared deep in thought.

I gave him the time he seemed to need, didn't push or speak.

"I'm sorry," he said at last.

"What? Why?" I asked.

"I apologized and you want to know why?"

I nodded.

"We've been over the whys. And you're not going anywhere," he said on a low rumble.

Yes, I was.

I needed to stand on my own two feet before I could succumb to any man ever again. Especially one who had such a potent effect on me and was as dominating as Gabe.

But I knew better than to think he would let me walk out without using the exact type of persuasion I couldn't resist, I thought. Which meant I'd have to play out the rest of the night, claim a headache, and go to sleep early.

First thing in the morning, or as soon as I could manage, I was going back to my original plan.

I was poised at yet another threshold in my life. Leaving Gabe was so much harder than walking out on Lance had been, but if I wanted Gabe to respect and not own me, I had no other choice.

Carly Phillips

Chapter Ten

Isabelle: Standing Strong, Being Me

It wasn't easy, and my heart hurt like hell, but when Gabe was called into work the next morning, I took the opportunity to escape. I left him a note, explaining the independence I needed in my life and why I had to leave him to find it.

I immediately contacted my old friend, boss, and mentor, Lisa. Her office was still in the same place, and she'd cried with relief on hearing my voice. The first night, I found myself a guest in her apartment, catching up on each other's lives. Lisa turned out to be a godsend and every inch a good friend. First, she offered to hire me as her assistant so I could slowly get back into design. I readily agreed. Although she'd obviously created the job as a favor, the first day back in the office, I took one look at her desk, her books, and the phone ringing off the hook, and I had little doubt she needed me.

She also gave me a place to live. She'd been seeing the same man for the last two years and stayed over at his place more often than not, and so she insisted I move into her apartment. We agreed on a fair rent, which she insisted helped her out since she'd basically moved in with Tom but hadn't wanted to give up her own place unless and until things were more permanent.

I was grateful, not thrilled about feeling like I was *taking*, but I wasn't stupid enough to begrudge the opportunity. I also knew Lisa. She didn't lie, and she didn't go easy. She was a tough boss, and I knew I'd work hard—and I did. I also went along on all her design appointments. She asked my advice, often used my vision, and before long, I grew comfortable asserting my opinions on color, fabric choice, and furniture placement. My school knowledge came back to me, and so did the two years of on-the-job training at Lisa's hand.

One morning not long after I'd left, a courier delivered an envelope for me at work. I signed, and the other man left. Inside, I discovered a check for the amount I'd had when I'd moved in with Lance, plus two years' worth of interest. To say I was stunned was an understatement, and I felt sure Gabe had something to do with the return of my funds. Which meant Lance wouldn't be pleased with him—or me. Despite me looking over my shoulder for a while after, Lance never surfaced in any way. And neither had Gabe. Even if he'd cared enough to push Lance into returning the money, he obviously wasn't interested enough to see me himself.

The first day, heck, even weeks after I'd left, I'd waited for him to come after me. A part of me had even hoped he would, not that I knew how I'd find the strength to resist him if he did. I didn't have to worry. He'd let me go much easier than I'd anticipated. In fact, he'd let me go completely. Either he'd respected my decision or I'd hurt or angered him to the point that he no longer cared. That was the thought that tortured me, the possibility that I'd caused Gabe pain in order to find my sense of self. I think some part of me believed he'd be persistent even as he tried to understand. I didn't think he'd let contact go. Then again, I'd left him. What else would a man with a healthy ego do?

There were times I wondered if he'd thought I was testing him by leaving and was angry that I'd played that kind of game with him. The truth was, I didn't know how to play games, not when it came to my heart. The fact remained, his silence reigned, as blatant and full of meaning as my parents', I thought, and a knife-like pain hit my heart.

Three months later, I still missed Gabe, all the while asking myself how I could miss a man I'd barely gotten to know. Yet he'd reached inside me with the things I craved most—understanding and true passion.

If I was honest with myself, and during this time of self-discovery, I'd forced myself to be nothing but, I also missed the sexual domination he'd exerted over me. Where Lance's control had been damaging and ego crushing, Gabe's had built me up in subtle but important ways. Just a few days with him and I'd felt stronger. Strong enough to leave the easy life he'd offered me and go out on my own just to prove to myself that I could.

This morning, as I settled into my desk and began checking messages, the familiar sound of Lisa coming through the doors had me looking up. She floated into the office. There was no other word to describe her arrival. Makeup perfect, blonde hair in symmetrical waves, she immediately came over to my desk, a huge smile on her face.

"Nice evening?" I asked, knowing Tom had told her to dress up because he was taking her somewhere special.

"Fabulous!" She flashed her hand at me, and I couldn't help but notice the big, sparkly engagement ring on her finger.

"Oh my God!" I squealed as only a friend could, jumped up, and hugged her tightly. "Congratulations!" I grabbed her hand for a better look. "Gorgeous."

"I know!"

I laughed, truly happy for her. Lisa had just turned forty, and she'd been beginning to think Tom would never propose, but she loved him too much to leave or issue an ultimatum. Clearly her persistence had paid off.

Instead of heading to her office and returning calls immediately as she usually did, Lisa perched herself on the corner of my desk. Never the kind of boss to define the workplace by hierarchy, she also didn't care that I was a good decade younger than her.

We'd clicked, therefore we were friends.

I settled back into my chair. "I'm thrilled for you," I told her.

"Thank you." She quietly assessed me with her vivid green eyes. "I'm glad you came back so I could share this with you. Not to mention the fact that you keep me organized."

I smiled at her. "I'm glad too." I'd missed the work, and I'd missed her friendship.

She leaned in close. "You know, I was fooled by Lance too."

I whipped my head up. She hadn't brought up Lance since the first night of my return, respecting that boundary, if not many others. I think she realized I needed time to heal, and she'd given me that. Apparently, with her engagement and happiness assured, it was time to focus on me.

My stomach churned, but I figured it was better to have the conversation and be done with it than to avoid it and let her push me until I revealed all.

"Lance really fooled you too?" I asked, surprised that *she* hadn't seen beyond the smooth exterior to the slime beneath either.

She nodded. "I would have tried harder to talk you out of quitting it—make that abandoning me here—but you were so happy. You loved him, and you wanted security. I knew you well enough to know that, and Lance seemed the perfect man to provide it."

At least I knew we'd both seen the same thing in Lance—in the beginning.

"I didn't like that you gave up your independence and career to be with him, but I respected that not all women wanted the same things from life. Although I knew I'd miss your talent."

I smiled. "I really did want to be happy with him. I wanted to make the home I never had but…" I smacked the side of my head and forced a smile.

"I admire you knowing what you wanted at such a young age. Nothing wrong with that. We aren't all cut out for career only." She glanced down at her ring as she spoke, making me think she'd done some reevaluating too.

"I should have realized when I called and couldn't reach you, and then when you didn't call me back—"

I held up one hand. "What?" To my knowledge, she had stopped calling me, cold turkey.

"When you started making excuses for getting out of our weekly lunches and had Lance tell me—"

"You *called* me?"

She nodded. "I called your cell. The number was disconnected, so I called Lance, and he promised to relay the message. After I did that twice, and he explained you'd made new friends and were too busy..."

Heat burned my cheeks. "God, I'm an idiot." In the beginning, he'd always come up with something I just had to do on the days I'd had plans with Lisa, but I didn't know he'd deliberately neglected to tell me she'd called. I should have realized. I shouldn't have let the friendship go so easily, but Lance had been there, encouraging me to move on.

Lisa waved away my self-blame. "It never dawned on me that he wasn't relaying the messages either. I just thought you were too busy with your new life and friends. And that was okay if you were happy, but I missed you." Her lips thinned. "I should have known you better. So you see? We were both duped. Take heart in that." Her kind gaze fell to mine.

"Thank you." Lisa was another person in my life I could count on, I thought, immediately realizing I was mentally including Gabe in that small group of two.

A lump filled my throat as it always did when I thought about Gabe.

"Anyway," Lisa said, her voice a welcome break from being in my own head, "we'll just find you your own man like Tom."

I hadn't told Lisa about my short time with Gabe before showing up again in her life. The pain had been too fresh, and I wasn't ready to admit I'd gone from one man's shelter directly to another. I also wanted to keep him, what I felt for him, to myself.

I shook my head at her. I didn't want a man like Tom. I didn't want just any man. I wanted the one I'd left behind.

But I didn't think going back was the right move, not with the months of silence between us. I'd taken some independent strides since leaving and had many steps still to come. I'd gotten what I needed—time alone to rebuild my life.

Too bad that life often felt so empty.

"We'll see," she said. "I'm just glad we had this talk."

"And I'm so happy for you." I glanced at her ring and smiled.

Lisa rose from her seat and held out her hand. "Messages," she said, back to business.

I blew out a breath, relieved to have some normalcy and no more talk bout my past. I handed her a stack of pink papers, mostly phone calls I'd retrieved from the answering machine.

She flipped through them. "Okay, I'm on these. I leave for Chicago on Wednesday," she reminded me.

"I remember." Lisa did a lot of travel for the initial consultation phase of a project and again during install.

Lisa headed for her office, and I returned to my work. A few hours later, my stomach growling, I headed out for lunch. Lisa's office was located near Cosi's, my favorite sandwich shop, and I ate outside, enjoying the sun on my skin, the light breeze blowing across my face and through my curls. I returned to the office refreshed and ready to work.

"Isabelle, I've been calling your cell for the last fifteen minutes!" Lisa said as soon as I stepped out of the stairwell. I'd taken to walking up the four flights, the trip up and down the only form of exercise I had time for.

"I'm here now. I didn't have any appointments scheduled. What's wrong?" I asked.

She shoved a folder into my hands. I glanced down. *Elite* was typed on the folder label. "New client?" I asked.

Lisa nodded, rushing me through the main entry and toward the conference room. .

"Then why aren't you taking them? You screen the clients, I work on the—"

"She asked for you," Lisa said.

I narrowed my gaze. "Nobody knows about me." I paused. "My designing abilities, I mean."

"Doesn't matter. This is a nightclub to end all nightclubs. Only the crème de la crème will go there, or should I say, be deigned entry. The woman in that room asked for you, so go!" Lisa shoved lightly on my back.

This whole scenario made no sense. Grasping the folder, I opened the door to the small conference room. "Lisa—" I glanced over to find my boss had disappeared.

I straightened my shoulders and headed inside, coming face-to-face with a petite brunette with dark blue eyes—eyes I'd seen not once but twice before. Eyes I wouldn't forget, even if this time they were in the face of a beautiful female.

"You must be Lucy Dare," I said, proud my voice didn't shake and betray my shock.

She smiled wide. "Isabelle."

I shut the door behind me and stared at the woman who looked so much like her brothers. I didn't know where to begin, so I started with the obvious. "Thank you."

"For what?" Lucy tipped her head to the side, curiosity—about all things *me*—oozing from her as she openly studied me.

"For letting me borrow your clothes." I blushed as I said it, but she deserved my gratitude. I'd come to Gabe with nothing but the clothes on my back, literally.

She waved a hand away. "What's mine is Gabe's to lend." She laughed but quickly sobered when she met my gaze. "He's never done that before. Ever."

Somehow I knew that. Believed her. Believed in him.

"What can I do for you?" I asked.

"What do you know about our club business?" she asked.

"Not much." I hadn't been around long enough to learn about Gabe's holdings.

"Good."

"Excuse me? You're obviously here to talk business, and you're glad I don't know much. How does that make sense?"

She smiled then. "I like you. And I can see why Gabe's hooked."

I narrowed my gaze. "I haven't spoken to him in three months."

She waved a hand. "It doesn't matter. Anyway, all of our current clubs are elite and exclusive. They cater to an upper-class clientele. Well-off people looking to blow off steam and pay a hefty fee to just walk in the front door."

Lucy, wearing a white pair of slacks, a yellow silk halter top, and high-heeled strappy sandals, began to pace as she spoke. Hands flying, animated, she was clearly in her element when discussing her business.

"All interesting facts, but it doesn't explain why you're here." I figured Lucy wanted to meet the woman who'd invaded her brother's life for a short time. Because I couldn't imagine that Gabe had pined for long—or at all—after I left.

"Because we've been given the opportunity of a lifetime. There's an exclusive island resort near the Bermuda Triangle. Eden."

I shook my head. "I haven't heard of it."

Her eyes lit up. "Not many people have. The only way to get to the island is to be invited by the Master, who is the host."

I shivered at the name *Master*, unsure of why.

"What does this have to do with me?"

"I'm getting to that. We've been offered first dibs to buy in and recreate one of our signature nightclubs there. Giving it its own unique stamp, of course. And I want you to manage the décor."

She held out a folder. "Inside are photographs of our clubs and other information about what makes Elite ... well, Elite. I want you to up the ante and help me create something beyond fabulous there," Lucy said.

"But—"

"No buts allowed," Lucy said, going on as if I hadn't objected. "We have to go visit the island, so your invitation is in the folder along with travel instructions and tickets. Since I assume you'll need time to buy island-appropriate clothing and organize yourself, you don't leave until Friday. There's an expense check in there for wardrobe since we're taking you out of your element here. It's a two-hour charter plane ride."

I blinked at the part about the expense check. "I already have summer clothing."

Lucy waved a hand dismissively. "Buy new ones anyway."

My head was spinning, both at the speed of her words and the scope and breadth of her request. No, not a request, a demand, making me wonder if this was her usual MO or something Gabe had concocted to see me again. My heart sped up in my chest at the thought.

"I'll meet you on the island," Lucy said, answering my question about Gabe's involvement. Even if he'd suggested me, this seemed to be Lucy's show and not her brother's. "Any questions?" she asked.

I shook my head.

"So you're in?"

As if I had a choice? Lisa might be my friend, but even she would fire me for turning down this opportunity. Still, none of this made any sense. I didn't have the expertise or the talent to take on this task even with the clearly formidable Lucy Dare to guide me.

"Lucy, don't get me wrong. I appreciate the offer. And please don't take this the wrong way, but if this is Gabe's version of charity, you can assure him I'm doing just fine."

Lucy tipped her head back and laughed. "Do you really think I'd risk handing over the biggest challenge of my career to someone my brother, at worst, feels sorry for or, at best, just wants to fuck?"

"Excuse me?" I tried to sound outraged, but the sad truth was, either was a valid possibility. And I appreciated her candor since I wanted to be the same in return.

Lucy propped a hip on the conference room table. "Look, my brother stepped in when my parents died. He made sure I wanted for nothing, from the material to the emotional, and I owe him for that. But even then, I wouldn't jeopardize our reputation on a whim of his. But you're no whim." Lucy Dare met my gaze, confidence oozing from her in a way I envied.

I turned and looked out the windows, confused. My usual state when it came to Gabe.

Lucy came up alongside me. Actually, she towered over my more petite frame, and her body was even more slender and perfect than her undergarments had led me to believe. Just as I had when wearing her clothes, I wanted to hate the lithe, beautiful woman who, from outward appearances, was everything I wasn't. But I knew appearances were deceiving, and life dealt blows and wounds nobody could see.

Besides, she was bouncy and nice and impossible to dislike. I let out a sigh. "Gabe was infatuated with me," I admitted. "If nothing else, I'm still a challenge to him." Not only because I left but because we'd never actually had sex.

She laughed. And laughed some more. "You really think that, don't you? Oh my God, you are perfect. Listen. My brother believes in you. And after years of watching him in action and learning, I believe in him."

I smiled at that, glad Gabe had Lucy in his life.

"Isabelle, he wants to give you this chance to shine. And I've looked into every client you had a hand in over the last three months. Not long, I know. But you do have design talent, and I have the experience to guide you. Everything in life comes down to who you know and opportunity." She picked up the

Stella McCartney handbag she'd placed on the table.

"I—"

"Don't decide now," Lucy said. "Spend the afternoon reading the information about our clubs and Eden. If you think you're up to the challenge, I'll see you on the island on Friday. If not, let me know, and I'll contact my second choice."

I picked up the folder, intrigued despite myself. "I'll seriously consider it," I promised her.

"It's been a pleasure, Iz," she said, a gentle smile on her lips.

The unexpected nickname set off a flurry of emotions and memories inside me, but before I could gather myself, Lucy Dare had walked out the door, leaving me behind with a folder. And a challenge.

One I sensed would eventually lead me back to Gabe. If I was brave enough to accept it.

Chapter Eleven

Gabe: Patience versus Sanity

Patience wasn't Gabe's strong suit. Three months had exhausted what little he had left. He waited for his sister's return, pacing his Madison Avenue office in the penthouse of their flagship hotel, staring out the wall of glass, as if he could see her petite form rushing up the street.

By the time Lucy let herself in—without knocking, Starbucks in hand—he was ready to throttle her. "Well?"

His sister settled into the chair across from his desk and propped her feet up on the polished wood. "I like her. She's feisty. And not too skinny. Oh, and she's not a bitch."

"Not what I meant, and you know it."

Lucy grinned. "She'll be there. I phrased it as a challenge. There's no way she won't rise to the occasion."

"If she's not—"

"Then you'll go after her like you should have done from the beginning," his sister said, a smug look on her face.

Gabe shook his head. "If I'd done that, she wouldn't trust me now."

"When she finds out you've kept tabs on her all this time, you think she'll trust you?"

He shrugged, but his skin felt too tight at the thought. "She'll understand," Gabe said.

She had to because he wasn't giving her up again.

Chapter Twelve

Isabelle: Paradise Awaits

I opened the invitation, my fingers gliding over the clearly expensive parchment-like paper, the words and information engraved on the page. The elegance and feel of the scroll writing and the almost demand-like phrasing to come to the island reminded me of Gabe, the deliberate way he went about things, the certainty he put into everything he did, and the sheer masculine perfection of the man. God, I missed him.

We'd barely been together at all, but the sense that I knew him and him me had remained during our time apart. Just as it had existed within me while I'd been with Lance. And now, even with Gabe gone from my life, knowing he'd easily let me go, I'd somehow felt his protection around me. Odd. Impossible. But still.

Swallowing hard, I pushed him out of my mind

and focused on work. The only reason I'd been invited to the tropical island was to create a nightclub, not imagine a reunion with the man I couldn't forget.

I researched Elite and discovered the clubs, both in Manhattan and the ones in various other cities like Las Vegas and South Beach, existed in a stratosphere the likes of which I'd never experienced. The challenge, to not just recreate the atmosphere but to exceed its luxury, was one I found impossible to resist. Still, I thought long and hard about whether or not I wanted a job that was handed to me courtesy of Gabe, who—I thought it best to remind myself—clearly was still avoiding direct contact. Even if it was what I'd told him I wanted, the fact he hadn't come after me still hurt. Talk about feminine indecision and wanting to have it both ways. I winced, not thrilled with myself at the moment.

Ultimately, I decided only a fool would turn down a once-in-a-lifetime opportunity. Elite wasn't just an exclusive nightclub. It was, for lack of a better metaphor, for the elite of the elite only, where celebrities like Rihanna, Beyonce, and Jay-Z were seen. Not only did you have to know someone to get in but you had to be willing to pay fifteen hundred to ten thousand dollars for the privilege of a table for the night. Yep, I'd be crazy to turn down the opportunity—as crazy as Lucy had been to entrust the job to me.

On Friday morning, I walked out of my apartment building and, just as the instructions indicated, a large stretch limousine waited out front.

"Isabelle Masters?" a man dressed in a chauffeur uniform asked me.

I nodded, and he held open the door for me to enter. I slid in, finding myself alone. I stretched my legs out in front of me and looked through the tinted windows, feeling like a celebrity as the driver took me to the airport for my trip to Miami, where I would switch to a charter for the short flight to Eden. Besides being in first class, which I would never have booked for myself, the first leg of the trip was uneventful.

Hours later, I was driven from the large main airport to a private airstrip. The plane, a seaplane, made me wish for a drink, a tranquilizer, or a potent combination of the two. The plane was too small, and the thought of landing on the water made my stomach dip with sheer nerves. I walked up the stairs, which I knew had been rolled out to the plane, and boarded.

The interior was small and confined, but before I could work myself into further panic, a woman walked out of what I knew was the cockpit.

"Isabelle?"

I swallowed over my fear. "Yes."

"I'm Joely, and I'm your pilot." She extended her hand, and I took it. Her no-nonsense grip was at odds with her entire appearance.

She was about my age with light brown, wavy hair, and her uniform, if you could call it that, consisted of khaki shorts and a black polo shirt. I could more easily picture her as an island guide than the woman who would be flying this plane. I played with the pearls at my neck, trying not to show my panic, which had only increased upon meeting her.

"Are you okay?" she asked perceptively.

I nodded. "Do you mind if I ask how old you are?" I blurted out.

She grinned. "Old enough to fly this baby, I promise. I'm a mechanic, and I have experience as a bush pilot. You're in safe hands." She waved hers in the air.

Her confidence inspired more in me. "Okay, then. I hope I didn't insult you."

She shook her head. "Nope. Don't worry, I get those questions a lot. So are you ready?"

I glanced around the empty inside of the vehicle. "I'm the only passenger?"

The other woman nodded. "It's a fast two-hour trip, so buckle up, and we'll get going."

I did as instructed. I still can't figure out whether I was grateful for the loud noise that surrounded us inside, preventing conversation, or if it frightened me more. I only know that I passed the two hours with a white-knuckle grip on the armrests, and I'd never been happier to see land.

The island I viewed out the window was nothing like I'd imagined. The greenery spread out as far as the eye could see, and jutting out from the lushness below, an Irish castle of gray stone sat looking majestic and regal in the distance.

I exited onto a long dock, grateful to be on the ground at last. I waved at Joely, who grinned and promised to return for me when my time was up. I had no idea when that would be.

Even though I was used to Manhattan in the summertime, the island humidity and heat swept over me, and I regretted choosing a pair of silk slacks, like I'd wear to work, and a tank top, which already clung to my breasts.

Alone on the dock, I fingered the pearls around my neck and looked around, relieved when a man strode toward me. As he drew closer, I realized he wore a cloak of some kind over his head, obscuring his face.

"Isabelle?" he said, sounding sure of my identity, as he extended his hand.

"Yes."

"Welcome to Eden."

"I knew immediately he was the elusive Master of

the island.

"Thank you," I said.

"Enjoy your time here."

I glanced up at the fantastical castle I'd seen from the air and smiled. "I'm sure I will." I turned to address him again, but strangely, he'd disappeared.

Before I could contemplate that oddity further, a woman approached from the pathway opposite the one the Master had taken. She wore a pair of simple silk khaki drawstring pants and a white sleeveless top, her name tag identifying her as Connie Hendrickson. Dark brown hair had been pulled into a work-friendly, island-necessary bun, keeping her hair off her neck.

She was attractive with a warm smile. "Isabelle," she said with the same familiarity everyone associated with this place had used. "Welcome to Eden. If you will come with me, I will show you to your room. Your bags will be brought up shortly."

"Has Lucy Dare checked in yet?" I asked, following her up a narrow, winding pathway.

She turned, her eyes narrowed in confusion. "I don't recognize that guest's name. The Master has placed you in the penthouse," she went on, as if my question hadn't been asked.

"There must be some mistake. I'm here to work. To help decorate the new club opening on the island. Elite?"

The other woman shook her head. I'd obviously asked another question she wasn't aware of the answer to. "I assure you there are no mistakes made here. You're in the penthouse." Again, she'd ignored my inquiry.

As we approached the castle, sliding glass doors immediately opened for us, and a blast of cool air assaulted me from inside. I gratefully stepped into what was clearly a lobby. It was darker than I'd expected, and I pulled my sunglasses off, allowing my eyes to adjust as I looked around. Dimly lit sconces adorned the mirrored walls, but I couldn't see myself in what must be tempered glass.

"We've recently upgraded the room keys, so if you'll just give me your hand," Connie said, capturing my attention.

She snapped a bracelet on my wrist and went on to explain. "Just line up the 'E' to the one on your door and the lock disengages. A little bit of technology we *borrowed* from Disney," she said with a smile.

I laughed. "This is as far from Disney as you can get," I murmured. "Unless you're in the Haunted Mansion."

Connie merely treated me to her smile. "This will allow you into the spa, the gym, and any other areas of the resort you might wish to visit while you are here."

I would be working, not lounging, but I decided

not to question her again. Surely I'd find Lucy soon, and all would be explained.

"Ready to see your accommodations?"

I nodded, and Connie gestured across the lobby. I followed her, surprised when we stopped near a stone wall. "Where is the elevat—"

Before I could finish my sentence, the *wall* opened, revealing the hidden lift. "Oh my."

We stepped on, and the doors closed behind us. "How thoroughly modern."

"Sensors," the other woman explained.

"Lift your hand and align the bracelet with the penthouse." I did as she asked, and soon we were in motion.

In complete awe, I wondered what awaited me next. I didn't have to wonder for long. The doors glided open.

"Your penthouse awaits," Connie said, sweeping her arm, gesturing for me to go first.

Unlike the darkened lobby, white floors and a wall of windows letting bright sunshine into the room beckoned, and I stepped directly into the luxurious suite. The enormity of the space hit me at once, and I shook my head, overwhelmed. Marbled floors, mirrored walls, plush carpeting in a living room with a cream couch and dark wood furniture. And a baby grand piano sitting in the center.

"No, this is wrong," I said, turning back to Connie, but the elevator doors finished closing on my words, and she'd disappeared.

Hesitantly and feeling like Alice in Wonderland, I made my way into the suite. Surely the other woman would return and tell me there had been an error and I was in one of the regular rooms on a lower floor. In the meantime, I decided to explore.

I glanced around, making my way to the bedroom, surprised to see that my suitcase had been brought up and placed on a luggage stand near the closet.

"That was fast." And odd, like everything else on the island so far.

Unsure of what to do with myself, especially since butterflies had once again had taken up residence in the pit of my stomach, I walked back to the foyer area. My hands went to the faux pearls at my neck, fingering them nervously. I'd bought them with the island-appropriate clothing for this trip.

I looked out the window, the view of the tranquil blue ocean and beautiful island below a panorama of indescribable beauty. Something I'd enjoy more if I understood what I was doing here.

I heard the whooshing sound of the elevator doors, and relief poured through me. "Lucy?" I asked, spinning around. Finally, everything would begin to make sense.

"Not Lucy." The familiar masculine voice wound its way through my veins, easing my fears, answering every unasked question.

Excitement flooded through me. It had been so long, and I'd missed him so much. To this day, it didn't matter that the time we'd shared together had been brief. To me, it meant everything.

He was just as I remembered, with his stern expression, features carved into what I considered perfection, full lips, strong jaw, and those intense eyes focused on me. A white dress shirt, sleeves rolled immaculately, and black slacks, with more casual shoes than his norm, completed the outfit.

He stared at me, his expression unreadable, maybe even vulnerable, and my heart thudded inside my chest. I studied him in return. His handsome face had occupied every dream I'd had, but he was here now. A reality. *My reality*, I thought, those sinfully sexy eyes eating me alive.

"Iz."

He held out his arms.

And my world suddenly righted itself once more.

I ran to him and jumped into his waiting embrace, wanting to be as close as possible. I clung to him, running my hands up his strong back, threading up through his silky hair. Hair that had grown longer since I'd seen him last.

There'd been many times in the last months when I had tried to convince myself the connection between us could not have been as strong as I remembered. The desire not as potent. That distance and might-have-beens were clouding my judgment and memory.

I'd been wrong.

Everything between us was solid, not a figment of my imagination, and right now, he was very real. Not just the thick erection snug against my core but the invisible thread that bound us together. Just then, his big hand cupped the back of my head, and he sealed his warm mouth over mine, and I knew at that moment, I'd come home.

He kissed me like I mattered, and the time melted away, and the kiss turned ravenous. Hungry. He devoured me, and him being Gabe, I expected nothing less. I merely wrapped my legs around his waist and held on, losing myself in the way he slicked his tongue inside my mouth, mimicking the physical act of making love. The thing we hadn't yet done.

He continued his assault, his fingers tight in my hair, tugging at my scalp, and my brain short-circuited from the pleasure. Real damned fireworks went off behind my eyes. No doubt about it, I was done for. Nobody else could ever live up to him.

He nipped at my lower lip, and I moaned, my pelvis grinding against him, seeking pressure to relieve the growing ache.

"Slow down," he said in a rough, harsh voice.

Of course he'd had to end the kiss to speak, and I whimpered at the loss of contact.

His glittering gaze met mine. "Just because I missed you doesn't mean I'm going to let you control things."

I'd missed the bossiness in his tone, not that I'd let him know that. Instead of arguing, I set about getting what I wanted, gliding my lips over his strong jaw, nuzzling my nose into the crook of his neck, where I could inhale his musky aftershave and lose myself in the masculine scent.

When he didn't take the bait, throw me on the couch, or slam me against the wall, I went for the kill, nibbling on his earlobe with my teeth. "I need you inside me," I said, my pussy throbbing with heat and damp with desire.

"And you'll have me when I say so."

"I hate your control," I muttered.

He grinned, his white teeth and handsome smile making me melt all over again. "You'll love it in a few minutes." He set me on my feet, but not before gliding me down the length of his body, allowing me to feel what I did to him.

My breasts might be heavy, my nipples tight as they rasped against my shirt, but his bulging erection told me that I wasn't alone in this hazy cloud of desire. His gaze never leaving mine, he gripped my pearls in one hand, pulling me forward with them, rubbing his nose against mine. "Behave and we'll both get what we want."

I managed a nod. My legs barely held me up, and the pull of the pearls at the back of my neck reminded me Gabe wouldn't let me fall. But apparently he would lead me to the bedroom by the necklace, and knowing what awaited me, I went along like a good girl. I briefly wondered if I'd lost my mind, but when he turned to me, those dark eyes glittering with need, I no longer cared.

"Too many clothes," he said, more to himself than to me.

He skimmed his hands along my bare arms, shoulder to wrist, and I shivered. He guided his palms up from my waist to beneath my armpit, taking my tank top along with him. Baring my breasts to his gaze.

He paused, deliberately grazing his thumbs over the underside of the soft mounds, over the lace of my bra, just allowing himself the luxury of touch and time. The pads of his thumbs reached inward, tracing the lines of my areolas but never touching the distended peaks just begging for the pressure of his fingertip. My clit throbbed, the dampness pooling between my legs overwhelming and embarrassing, but I wasn't going to mention it. I didn't want him to stop, even if his maddeningly slow pace might kill me, and I shifted restlessly on my feet.

He reached up and tweaked one nipple hard, and I squeaked aloud, then sucked in a shallow breath. "What was that for?"

"You left me, you made me wait months, and now it's going to be at my speed, not yours."

"Whatever happened to wham, bam, thank you, ma'am?" I asked grumpily, thinking of Lance. He might not have satisfied me all that much, but at least I didn't have to suffer through such intense arousal and near pain of wanting and being denied.

Gabe's indigo eyes narrowed. "Is that what you expect from me? From us? You have to know I'd put your pleasure first."

And I had to admit the pain had morphed into something different. A warm pleasure suffused my body, and as if there was an invisible connection between my nipples and my sex, there was a direct correlation to the need he'd inspired with that hard pinch.

I relaxed at his words. This wasn't about torturing me, this was about pleasure. Mine. And hopefully his. I felt my shoulders dropping, my breathing slowing.

"That's better," he said in a husky voice. He slid my top up and over my head, then paused to fold it and place it on the dresser.

I waited obediently, allowing my mind to empty. He returned to me, those dark eyes intense, and he unhooked my bra, slowly easing the lace material down the slope of my breast, revealing my lush curves and the darkened nipples, aroused and erect. For him.

He sucked in an approving breath. "You're so fucking gorgeous, Iz."

My lashes fluttered down. I couldn't meet his gaze any more than I could believe him. Yes, he wanted me. I still hadn't figured out exactly why or what he saw in me that my long-term, live-in lover hadn't.

A strong hand tilted my chin up. "Eyes open. You can't believe what I'm telling you if you don't watch my face when I say it."

I swallowed hard. Looked into his gorgeous face, his expression taut.

"You can't think this is easy for me, denying myself the pleasure of my cock sliding into your soaking-wet pussy *now*."

Another thing I wasn't used to. The blunt words. The honest sex talk. I felt myself blush.

"I want you so badly I ache with it." He pulled me flush to him, his erection so hard and thick against my belly.

I lost the ability to breathe.

"I just want you to know what you mean to me,"

he continued, his honest words lulling me into submission. "This isn't some one-night stand. Wham, bam, thank you, ma'am." He growled the words in disgust. "You deserve much more than that."

I sighed. So gruff sometimes, yet so sweet at others. All part of this enigmatic man.

He placed my bra with my top, returned and unbuttoned my slacks. My belly quivered at his deft touch. Pants slid down my thighs, my panties along with them, both pooling at my feet.

My heart pounded hard in my chest. I fought the embarrassment of being naked while he was so elegantly dressed. I stepped out, and he patiently bent down, folding the pants and adding them to the pile.

"Shoes?" I asked, gesturing to the sandals I'd chosen, thong-style with glittering rhinestones.

To my surprise, he knelt and slid them off my feet. Those, he placed on the floor near the dresser. My meticulous man. I bit the inside of my cheek. Not mine … I wasn't sure what this was. Nor did I know what I wanted it to be.

But when his hand came down on my shoulder, nothing mattered beyond now.

I reached for the pearls, intending to pull them off too.

"Leave them. I want to fuck you with nothing but those pearls between us."

He was so sure of himself, so sexy, and I was … a lot inexperienced and even more naïve. I couldn't imagine what he wanted from me and was even less certain I could satisfy him. My history with Lance had proven that.

"Okay, enough thinking."

He lifted me into his arms as if I weighed nothing, dropping me onto the bed in one smooth move. Without warning, he had both my wrists over my head, and somehow, he secured me to the headboard using the bracelet on one hand and cuffs I hadn't noticed before.

"You're kidding."

"Not one bit."

"Don't you want me to touch you too?" I asked, confused.

"Next time. After I've had my fill and know it won't be the rushed affair you seem to desire." He began unbuttoning his shirt, revealing tanned skin, a sexy, liberal sprinkling of dark chest hair, and a six-pack that spoke of hours in the gym.

Watching him as he hung the shirt over the chair, the muscles in his back and forearms flexing as he moved, I let out a moan.

He turned. Grinned. Eyes on mine, he undid his pants, slipping them off, no underwear to be concerned about hindering him in any way. And then he stood before me nude, his thighs as strong as the rest of him, his cock larger than I'd imagined, thick and long and completely erect.

"Oh God."

"I thought we'd clarified that last time. Just me."

"There is no *just* about you," I muttered under my breath, my nipples erect and clearly as impressed with his body as my mind.

He chuckled before striding over, completely confident in his nudity—and why wouldn't he be? He was strong and well defined, while I was bound, my breasts thrusting upward for his viewing, my soft and slightly rounded stomach there for him to see.

Could this be any more mortifying?

I felt the dip of the bed as he joined me, the grip of his hands as he pulled my legs apart and stared down, a slow smile spreading across his face.

Just what did he see? I wondered.

Without warning, he slapped my pussy, the same way as he'd done back in New York, and I yelped. "Either you stop thinking and enjoy or I'm going to bind your legs as well. I'll turn you over, tie you to the bed, and spank your ass until you can't think of anyone or anything but me. And what I make you feel."

My eyes opened wide—both at his words and the warmth gushing between my thighs.

"You like the idea," he said, trailing a finger through my sex and the moisture there.

I moaned at the slick touch that wasn't enough to satisfy the ache.

"What's going on in that head of yours that you can't be in the moment?"

I stared up at the ceiling, unable to face him. "It's just … you're you, and I'm the woman who couldn't satisfy—"

"The asshole who has no place in this bedroom," he said harshly. "Trust me, you wouldn't be here if I didn't want you. You're beautiful. Perfect." His admiring tone couldn't be anything but real. He slid a hand over my stomach and left his palm there. "You're round where you should be, soft where I need you to be. And I don't want you worrying about it again."

"Yes, sir," I said jokingly. I'd have saluted if my hands were free.

His eyes merely darkened, and his lips came down hard on mine.

I sighed into his mouth and reveled in the possessive kiss, his tongue swirling around, owning every inch of the deep recesses of my mouth. He tasted dark and sexy, like Gabe, the man who'd spoiled me for any other man. He knew how to kiss, and as much as I could do it for hours with him, my body was protesting the lack of touch, arching up off the bed without my permission.

He gripped my hips, holding me down. He trailed his lips from one side of my mouth to the other, then slid them downward, easing over my jaw, where he paused to inhale, much as I'd done to him.

"God, you smell good." He continued down until his gorgeous face was between my breasts, where he pressed a kiss against my sternum, his lips hovering over my skin. My body buzzed with anticipation. Finally, his big hands cupped one breast, raising it so he could lick at my nipple, teasing, suckling, his light touch at odds with the strong way he held my breast, his fingertips digging into my soft flesh. Such a contradiction, the bite of his fingers and light thrash of his tongue. The sensations were almost too much to bear, moisture pooling between my thighs, my clit pulsing with need.

Yeah, that took care of the thinking problem. All I could do was feel. He worked one breast thoroughly before moving to the other, his warm mouth and talented teeth and tongue arousing me to the point of insanity.

I thrashed on the bed, needing him to fill me, needing to come. "Please," I moaned, pulling at my bindings, my hips rising in a plea of their own.

"Please what, kitten?"

My entire body trembled at the endearment. "Please make me come."

He covered my pussy with his full hand. Warm heat suffused me at his possessive touch. "How? Tell me what you need."

"You." I arched my hips, and he slid one finger inside. "I need you." In and out, he teased me, but it wasn't quite enough. "More."

"Like this?" He added a second finger to the first. Hooked his fingers forward, hitting my sweet spot.

"Oh yes." He pumped in and out, but it still wasn't enough. "No. More." Tears filled my eyes, the begging so out of character for me it was hard to do. It hurt to ask for anything when I usually got so little from people in return.

He met my gaze, brushing my hair from my eyes. "Shh. I'm going to take care of you." He slid down my body until I felt his harsh breath over my sex.

This time, he didn't make me ask or beg, he simply drew me into his warm, delicious mouth. I closed my eyes and gave myself over to him, the hot glide of his tongue over my sensitive folds, the thorough way he ate at me like he'd never have enough. But most of all, the way he focused on that one spot that needed him most.

Hands gripped my hips hard, his tongue lashed at my clit, coaxing more of a response from me than I'd believed myself capable of. I shook, I saw stars, I felt myself climbing up, up, reaching for something far bigger than me, something not even a handheld toy could achieve, never mind another man. And then I was there, the climax shaking me to my core.

I cried out, incoherent words, low guttural moans as he kept me coming beneath his mouth and stayed with me until the large quake became smaller tremors and I lay beneath him, my body spent.

Except his wasn't, and as soon as I felt the nudge of his hard cock against me, I opened my eyes, wanting to see him as he finally took me.

"There's nothing between us," his said in a gruff voice.

"There's been nobody since … you know, and considering everything before, I've also been checked."

A muscle ticked in his jaw at the mention of Lance. "And there's been nobody since you walked into my apartment. I'm clean."

Tears pricked my eyes, and suddenly he was there, thrusting inside, taking away all thought and concern. There was only Gabe, big and hard, easing his way inside me.

"You're tight," he said, his voice shaking along with his muscular arms as he held back. "But you feel so damned perfect."

The burn as he pushed deeper spoke of Gabe, our connection. I welcomed it, knowing how much I wanted to give to this man. The thought scared me. It came with the fleeting reminder of how much was still unsaid between us. But then he began a steady pumping, in and out, until he'd lodged in deep.

I felt him. "Gabriel," I moaned, unable to keep the feelings inside.

"Oh, Iz." His self-control fled, and he fucked me. There were no other words as he took me hard and fast, easing out, slamming in deep. All the while holding my gaze, not letting me look away as he possessed my body, his arms braced, enabling him to thrust in and out, bringing us both higher and higher. I'd never been on such a precipice before, and I needed to touch him. I tugged at the bindings on my arms, groaning when I couldn't release myself. He reached out a hand, did something, and then I was free to roam my hands over his broad shoulders, the muscles flexing as he drove in and out of me, taking what he wanted and giving me everything in return.

I shook, felt the beginnings of an orgasm I wasn't sure I could handle. Not with those intense blue eyes boring into me, making me vulnerable and even needier. Before I could think, he changed position just a touch, and he hit that spot. The one his fingers easily found when he wanted me to soar.

“Oohh,” I let out a long, embarrassing wail.

It merely spurred him on. He hooked an arm around my back, pulled me to a sitting position, and then I was facing him. Looking into his eyes as he ground himself into me and came hard.

My name on his lips triggered my release and brought me along with him.

Chapter Thirteen

Isabelle: Being Me

The afterglow took a long time to fade. I think I slept or at least catnapped. That was okay, since I woke up wrapped in warmth, and I was in no rush to break away from the strong arms holding me tight. He slept beside me, his big body lax, obviously finding the same ease with me as I did with him. But he gave me more. I felt so protected when I was with Gabe, so right. I could wake up like this every morning, I thought, and cut off my musings. I had no right to think beyond the here and now. Time, I needed it to make sure I didn't jump without thinking, like I tended to do when it came to men. To the idea of security.

"Isabelle?" a female voice called out from the living room.

I jumped at the intrusion.

"Isabelle? It's me, Lucy! I thought I could welcome you to the island, have a drink, and we could talk about—" Lucy halted in the doorway, shutting up as she took in the sight of me. In bed with her brother.

"Oh my God." I crawled lower into the bed.

"Go away, Lucy."

"I thought I'd welcome her, Gabe. I didn't think you'd jump her the minute she arrived."

I cringed. Gabe merely glanced down, making sure he was covered.

"Actually, she jumped me." He grinned, and I sank lower, managing to elbow him in the side for his sarcasm.

"Fine. I'm going. Since it's near dinnertime, why don't we just meet tomorrow. Isabelle, you can text me when you're ready to work on the club."

The club. The reason I thought I'd been summoned here. The reminder brought the real world crashing back.

I waited for Lucy to disappear before sitting up in bed. "This really was a setup. Invite me here to work on the club as a pretext to getting me into bed. I told Lucy I didn't have the experience, but she assured me I could handle it. I knew you'd had a hand in it, but I didn't think…" I shook my head. "Never mind. I'll see if Joely can bring me back to Miami first thing in the morning."

His hand gripped mine. "Did I set you up to come here to meet me? Yes. Because you wouldn't have come otherwise."

I shook my head, biting down on my lower lip. "I needed the time apart," I said. "It was the only way to get through each day and build myself into a worthy woman. Instead of respecting that, you set up a way to get me a job."

"You're wrong about one thing. You were always a worthy woman. Worthy of a lot more than the hand you were dealt. Success is all about who you know and what you make of the opportunity."

"You and Lucy are drinking the same Kool-Aid."

He cupped the back of my head in his hand, subtly controlling my ability to move. My body responded as if we hadn't just made love … had sex. An insistent throb began low in my belly. I didn't recognize the woman whose sexual need was so strong, who wanted … so much.

"The fact is, I gave you as much time as I could take. Patience is not my strong suit in general. When it comes to you? It's nonexistent," he said, his voice a guttural rumble.

"You let me go so easily. I thought you'd forgotten me." I blinked up at him. "And before you say it, I know. It's a contradiction to think that way considering I'm the one who walked out on you."

His perpetually stormy eyes darkened further. "I gave you what you wanted—what you needed—for as long as I could. I always will. But make no mistake. You were never alone."

Whatever he meant by that, I wasn't sure I needed specifics. I'd always sensed that if something went wrong, Gabe would be there. He wouldn't have let me fall. He'd provided an inherent safety net I hadn't known about, and that was the key. I. Hadn't. Known. I'd been on my own.

But the truth of this trip settled over me, dulling the good feelings. "So the job? I can't imagine Lucy really needs me. She's put together every club you already own." So why had I come here?

He shook his head. "Lucy's in charge of the décor in the clubs. She looked at the portfolio of the things you've done with Lisa, and along with my recommendation, she wanted to give you a chance."

I blinked. "The opportunity is real?" I asked warily.

"As real as you want it to be."

"In other words, if I want to come back home with you and play house, you'd prefer it."

"Not prefer. I want whatever makes you happy."

Lance had said the same thing, and yet slowly, subtly, he'd taken away everything I'd ever loved.

I realized he'd pulled me into his arms, and I was wrapped in him, just the way he liked things. I felt so safe, so wanted. How, when he'd manipulated the situation to get me here? My heart and my sense of self-worth warred with each other.

"I want you happy, but make no mistake. I want you with me. And this time? You aren't going to disappear."

I shook my head. "You're playing me, and I don't like it. So don't ask me to make any promises about the future."

He exhaled hard, and a few uncomfortable moments passed. "Then make a promise for now. Stay with me on Eden."

I didn't know how long he meant or what he intended for us while we were here. I did know that despite the circumstances, I wanted to decorate that club as much as I wanted this time with him. Standing on my own two feet had felt great—but I felt even better here in Gabe's arms.

I didn't trust that he'd allow me the freedom I needed to be me in the real world. And that scared me as much as leaving him did.

Still, I managed a nod. I wasn't going anywhere. For the moment.

"Are you hungry?" he asked.

"I worked up an appetite," I said, somewhat cheekily. After all, my body still hummed with aftershocks of pleasure, and I was deliciously sore.

He groaned and pulled me into a long kiss. We didn't eat or think about food for a long, long while.

* * *

Isabelle: Elite

I woke up the next morning to find Gabe already gone from the bed. I washed up and pulled a robe over my naked body. The man didn't like to sleep with clothes, and he'd been insatiable throughout the night. He blamed our long time apart, and I couldn't deny everything he made me feel either. Hot, achy, and wanted and needed.

I headed into the kitchen area to find him on the phone. Wearing a pair of gym shorts, he barked orders at the unlucky person on the other end and paced back and forth as he spoke.

He turned, caught sight of me, and his gaze warmed. "Just take care of it," he said, disconnecting the call.

"Everything okay?" I asked.

He nodded. "Just business."

I walked over to the coffeepot, which had obviously been delivered earlier, and poured myself a cup of hot coffee, added milk and one artificial sweetener packet before turning toward him. "Speaking of business, I'd like to find Lucy and see the site where

Elite will be."

"I thought we could spend the day seeing the island. Work will be there when we're finished."

I raised an eyebrow, knowing I had to put my foot down now or this was never going to work between us. "Or I can see Elite this morning and free myself up for you the rest of the afternoon." I drew a long sip of the coffee, needing the caffeine to begin flowing through my veins, especially if I was going to go up against Gabe's determination.

I saw the argument going on within him before his shoulders relaxed and he obviously gave in. "I'll call Lucy and have her take you down."

I blinked. No way had I thought it would be that easy. "Really?"

I placed my now-half-empty cup down on the counter and strode over to him, winding my arms around his neck. "That wasn't so difficult, was it?" I pressed against his warm body, rubbing my cheek against his.

A low rumble escaped from his chest. "You're making it harder," he muttered.

I laughed. He'd given me what I wanted. From the thick erection poking at my stomach, he needed something too. I could afford to be generous. And since he'd denied me the ability to really play with him last night, I wanted to now.

I slipped my hand into the waistband of his shorts and grasped his cock.

"You're playing a dangerous game," he warned me. "If you want to get going, you'd better do it before I change my mind."

"I didn't say it had to be this second," I murmured, pulling his shorts down at the same time I went to my knees.

I glanced up at him. His eyes were dark, his jaw tight. "You need to relax," I said, gliding my hand up and down his long, thick length, trying not to be too overwhelmed by the size.

Lance, thank God, hadn't liked oral sex—in either direction—and to be honest, neither had I. Gabe had completely altered my perception of the act, and I wanted to give this to him. I needed to.

His hand came to rest on the top of my head at the same time I leaned forward and licked at the round head, already leaking. He groaned, and his touch turned into a firm grip on the back of my head. I moaned at his commanding touch at the same time I encased as much of him as I could inside my mouth.

I can't say I knew what I was doing, especially not in this position. The few times with Lance had been early in our relationship, and he'd been lying on the bed. Instinct had guided me to my knees with Gabe, and instinct had me licking and sucking him now.

"You're so damned good with that mouth, baby," he said, the praise in his tone only making me want to keep going, to please him more.

I pulled him in deeper, inhaling his rich, musky scent as I slid my tongue up and down the length, grazing him lightly with my teeth.

He groaned and thrust forward, the head of his cock hitting the back of my throat. My eyes watered, but I wanted to give him as much pleasure as he'd given me.

"Relax, kitten. You can take me if you do."

His words and the certainty in his voice both inspired me and eased my sudden panic, and I did as he said, surprised when, with his next thrust forward, I was able to relax and swallow around him.

His big body shuddered, and his hand tightened in my hair. A steady pumping of his hips followed, and I managed to lick, suck, and take him deep each time.

Above me, he swore, shook, and I knew he was close. Without warning, he pulled out, reached down, and lifted me into his arms. "What's wrong?"

"Not coming anywhere but inside you," he muttered, backing me into the wall. He lifted my short robe and slammed into me on a rough groan, filling me completely.

I closed my eyes at the sheer rightness of the moment, but he tugged at my hair. "Look at me."

No sooner had I opened my eyes than he pulled out and thrust back in, picking up a fast and furious rhythm that had me bucking between Gabe and the wall. Pressure built quickly, no doubt from the sheer intensity of how much he wanted me. It was intoxicating, knowing I made him so out of control and that I responded in exactly the same way.

I felt him, so big and hot inside me, pounding hard on my clit and hitting that spot inside me with every thrust home. I was so close, light-headed, everything whirling around me, as my world narrowed to just this. Me and Gabe and the perfection we created.

He twisted his hips, and I barely recognized the sound that came from my throat. "Oh God. More, harder." I dug my nails into his back, pulling him into me, grinding myself against him as I spun out of control, pleasure overtaking every inch of me, every pore. "Gabe!"

"Fuck, Iz, need you," he groaned, his sweat-slickened body gliding up against mine. "Need you."

I pulled at his hair as I climaxed again—or was it still—and felt the hot spurt of him as he came inside me, finally stilling. His body held me in place, my breath coming in long gasps, his breath hot against my neck. Eventually he lifted me into his arms, slowly eased me to the floor, waiting until my legs were steady enough to hold me.

I excused myself and went to the bedroom to fix myself up. When I returned, he'd pulled his shorts back on and led me outside to the deck that overlooked the beach. A gorgeous stretch of sand extended to the clear blue water beyond. In front of me, breakfast had been laid out for us. Fruit and croissants and, blessedly, more coffee.

He pulled me onto his lap, wrapping me in his arms. Even though it was hot outside, the ocean beyond provided a breeze, and I didn't mind being cuddled against him. In fact, I loved it.

I leaned against Gabe's chest and relaxed, breathing in the salty air. "It's gorgeous here."

"I'm glad you came."

He sounded like the admission hadn't come easily. "Me too." And I was. If we could find a compromise that let me feel independent, maybe we had a chance.

My stomach chose that moment to growl unattractively. I squirmed to move away, but he held fast. He picked up a piece of fruit and held it for me. "Open."

I blinked. "Gabe, I can feed myself."

"Humor me," he said in a gruff voice. "I called Lucy, and she's going to be here soon, at which point, she'll keep you occupied for who knows how long." He dangled the juicy-looking melon from his fingers.

I smiled and ate the cantaloupe, making sure to nip at his fingers as I did. "Watch yourself or you'll end up skipping breakfast," he said on a growl.

I grinned. "Promises, promises."

He shook his head and held up another piece. The meal continued in comfortable silence, odd considering a man was feeding me and I'd had more sex in the last twelve hours than in my entire life.

"Tell me about your family," Gabe said, taking me completely off guard.

"What? Why?" I never spoke about them. I didn't see the point, and if nothing else, it was embarrassing to explain how unwanted I'd always been.

"What exactly do you think I want from you, Isabelle? If it was just sex, I could get that anywhere," he said, a touch of hurt sounding beneath the gruff words.

I glanced down. "I don't know."

He blew out an obviously frustrated breath. "I want to know you better. So talk to me. You had no one to turn to when you left Daltry. I want to know why."

I pulled up the walls that had kept me protected for most of my life and spoke in a detached voice. I liked to pretend my past belonged to someone else. It didn't hurt as much that way. "I was a mistake. My parents didn't want me, so I don't have a relationship with them. What time is Lucy coming to get me?" I asked, attempting to pull off his lap.

He wasn't letting me go. "I'm sorry. That's an awful thing to know."

"Yes, it is. But at least I know what to expect from people. I mean them," I amended, not wanting him to realize how deep some hurts ran.

He stroked my hair, probably in an effort to get me to relax against him again, but he'd destroyed the moment.

"I'm assuming that when Daltry turned on the charm, you believed you'd found the one thing you were missing. Someone who cared. Who loved you."

A painful lump rose in my throat. "I don't want to talk about this."

"I do," he said in that compelling voice. "Because I also have a feeling this is exactly why you don't believe I have your best interests at heart. Because nobody before me ever has."

Real tears threatened, then fell, splashing on his golden chest. "Damn you," I muttered. "Do you want to talk, Gabe? Do you want to tell me who *she* was?" I looked up, wanting to see his expression.

"She who?" His voice sounded cold, and I shivered.

What a joke, I thought. Exactly as I'd thought, he pushed me to open up but was unwilling to do the same. "You know who. The last stray you took in."

I remembered his brother's words in the police

station. They'd stayed with me and helped me find the courage to leave. I didn't want to be anyone's pet project. Someone he could keep and feed and feel sorry for.

"She has nothing to do with us."

"Oh, but my past, my parents, do?" I pushed hard against his chest, and this time he let me go. I started for the sliding door to the penthouse.

"Isabelle, come back here." His tone said he expected me to obey.

"I told you I do what *I* want. And if you can't share in return, it doesn't matter what you want from this relationship," I informed him. "It's over." I stormed inside only to see the elevator doors open and Lucy step out.

"Good morning," I muttered and headed directly for the master bedroom. I took a fast shower, then dressed in a bathing suit and cover up, with a pair of flip-flops that looked as expensive as they were.

Stupid, stupid, stupid, I thought. I shouldn't have spent the money. I knew it had belonged to Gabe. I shouldn't even have come here.

Without looking at the terrace, where I heard Lucy and Gabe's raised voices, I hit the elevator button. If the man couldn't open up about himself, how did I expect to have a relationship with him, never mind maintain my independence? What I wanted from Gabe was … what?

The doors opened. I stepped into the open elevator and turned in time to meet Gabe's shuttered gaze before the closing doors cut off contact. I headed for the privacy of the beach. I wanted to be alone. Later, I would have to find someone who could direct me to Joely and a way to get off this island.

But as I walked through the hotel, the question in my head remained. What did I want from him? Unfortunately, I knew. I wanted what I'd been pushing down and away since I'd realized Lance was a selfish prick who would never love me. I wanted a family. A man who loved me unconditionally, and kids we loved, who were wanted the way I never had been. And even if I'd never expressed it or even allowed myself to formulate the thought before, I'd wanted it with Gabe.

Chapter Fourteen

Gabe: Protect and Defend

"You idiot!" Lucy yelled at him. "Only you could drive away a woman on an island called Eden!"

Gabe pinched the bridge of his nose and groaned. "Stay out of it, Lucy."

She laughed. "As if. If I leave it to you, you'll screw up a sure thing. What's happened? What did you do to her?"

Well, he'd started by digging into her painful childhood and forcing her to open up, and he'd ended by shutting her out when she'd asked him to do the same.

"Okay, I'll guess. You told her you'd been married?"

"I wouldn't tell her anything," he muttered.

Lucy clapped slowly, applauding his idiocy. "I get it. She asked, you shut down."

If he didn't explain, she'd just keep talking, and he already had a splitting headache. "I pressed about her past and forced answers—"

"And then you wouldn't give up anything in return. Oh, good job, big brother." She picked up a piece of cantaloupe and popped it into her mouth.

All Gabe could think about was Isabelle sitting on his lap, curled into him as if she belonged, allowing him to take care of her. Yes, he had this caretaker streak, but it wasn't about strays. It was more about making sure the people he loved got what they needed, just like he'd done for Lucy and Decklan when their parents had … died. His thoughts careened to a stop, backing up to one word. *Love.*

Did he love Isabelle?

Want, desire, an all-consuming need to protect and defend. He hadn't touched a woman since she'd come into his life. Really come into his life that night at the police station. In the three months alone, he'd turned Naomi away when she'd tried for a second chance, something he wouldn't be informing Isabelle of.

He hadn't used a condom, and she hadn't mentioned birth control either. In his mind, it hadn't mattered. He didn't plan on letting her go.

So did he love her?

Hell yes, he did.

"God, I have to tell her the truth, don't I?" he

asked his unusually quiet sister.

She shrugged and snagged another piece of fruit. "Just don't screw it up. I like her. And given the women you normally hang out with? I don't want you to lose this one. She's special."

He blew out a long breath. "I agree."

"And she likes you for you. Not your money or power."

He grinned. "She does, doesn't she?" He rose to his feet.

"Where are you going?" Lucy asked.

"To shower, change, and find my girl."

Chapter Fifteen

Isabelle: A Day of Revelations

Although I intended to find the beach or the pool, a private place to unwind and think, I hit the wrong floor on the elevator and ended up on the bottom level beneath the main lobby area. The sign across from the open doors said CLUB, so I decided to look around and came upon the original club that had been shut down. Obviously Elite would open here, and I decided to look around.

I pushed open the doors. The place was dark, just a few lights marking my way. The tables, chairs, and even the countertop were visibly old and scarred, the floors dingy. The place needed a complete overhaul, and my creative juices were already flowing. I couldn't wait to hear what Lucy had in mind. No matter that I'd initially been upset, I wasn't stupid.

I understood how the world worked. Connections

and money ruled. They opened doors. So Gabe had introduced me to Lucy, who probably didn't need my advice, but she was willing to accept my input anyway. That would give me the opportunity to prove my ability, and from there, it was up to me to make the most of it. No matter what happened between myself and Gabe.

With the return of that unpleasant thought, I decided to really head to the beach. Maybe I could find a place to get a fruity drink and fall asleep—and not think. Thinking only hurt. Gabe wanted me, of that I was certain. But if he didn't care to let me in, to share his past, mere wanting wasn't enough.

Luckily, I found the beach easily. To my surprise, the long stretch was empty, nobody around but me and the guy who brought me towels for my chair and the occasional waitress who came by serving drinks. Soon I had my cover-up off, the sun baking my skin, and a piña colada in my hand.

I closed my eyes and breathed in deeply, enjoying the utter peace of the moment, not allowing any thoughts to intrude. How often did I have the chance to do absolutely nothing and enjoy it? I wasn't sure how much time had passed when a shadow suddenly covered my sun.

I blinked up to find Lucy standing over me.

"I want to talk, and we don't have much time," she

said before I could utter a word. "Gabe's showering and then coming to look for you."

"What can I do for you, Lucy?"

"Glad you asked." She settled herself on the side of my chair, pushing my legs over to make room. "You know our parents died when I was sixteen, right? Gabe was twenty-one, and he singlehandedly took over. He handled the hotels, expanded, and branched into nightclubs. He made sure Decklan didn't have to do anything except finish college and become a cop, and he raised me, and I wasn't easy." She grinned, but the seriousness of the conversation wasn't lost on me.

"I know he's a good man."

"Well, he's also a tortured one. Once he got me off to school, Gabe got married."

I sat up in my seat. "What? Gabe was married?"

"Lucy!" Her brother barked out her name like a command.

Lucy rose to her feet, going toe-to-toe with Gabe, although she only came up to the middle of his chest. "At least something's out in the open now. You have no choice but to explain everything."

"And you didn't think I was coming down here to handle things myself?"

"I just didn't want you to be able to chicken out."

Gabe gritted his teeth and shook his head, but I couldn't help but laugh. "I knew I was missing something by not having siblings."

Lucy glanced at me and winked. "We can meet later and talk about what I have in mind for the club. Something tells me my brother is going to keep you occupied for a while." With a grin, she strode off, her long hair swinging behind her.

"I'm going to throttle her," Gabe muttered.

I lay back down, ignoring him. I hadn't for one second forgotten I was angry with him. If he was going to talk, he was going to do it because he wanted to, not because I begged him to or his sister pushed him into it.

"Iz." He sat down where Lucy had been, his muscular leg warm and hard against mine.

I raised a hand over my eyes like a visor to block out the harsh rays, met his gaze, and waited for him to speak.

"You're burning. Do you have sunscreen on?" he asked in that protective voice that softened my insides.

"Yes." I snapped my eyes closed once more.

He groaned. "We lost our parents in a car accident on the way home from my college graduation."

I sucked in a shallow breath. He was talking, and I hadn't expected him to dive right in. Nor did I have to imagine the guilt he must have felt. I only had to look into his tortured expression to know. I placed my hand over his, understanding he wouldn't want pity or sympathy but determined to provide it anyway.

"I immediately stepped up to be there for Lucy. She was sixteen and needed a firm hand. Deck was nineteen, and he helped, but he was in school. He never wanted anything to do with hotels or business. Law enforcement was all he ever desired, and I didn't want him to lose that. So I became the head of the family and made sure everyone got what they needed."

I watched him as he spoke, so self-contained and sure of what he'd had to do. But he'd been so young, I thought. Like I'd been when I left home, but I'd had to take care of just myself. He'd held a world of responsibility on his shoulders.

"Who gave you what you needed?" I asked.

He blinked at that. And shrugged. "At first, I didn't think about it, and then I met Krissie. I was working ungodly hours, and all I saw was someone to share my life with. I thought it would help ease the pain and loneliness."

"What happened?" I asked into the yawning silence. I could tell this was where he didn't want to continue.

"I should have looked more closely because she needed … so much. More time, more affection, more of everything than I had to give. Especially back then."

I expelled a long breath. "That's why Decklan called me another stray."

Gabe inclined his head. "Deck only saw it from the outside. He didn't see my faults."

I narrowed my gaze. "What faults? You were keeping an eye on your college-age sister, sustaining your father's business while learning it at the same time, and taking over nightclubs. I'm assuming she had a wonderful life? A roof over her head? You loved her?"

"I thought I did."

I let that go. "So what was she missing?"

"Everything? Nothing was enough. No time I managed to get home for dinner, no short vacation... She eventually turned to another man." He shook his head. "By the time I found out, we'd grown so far apart I couldn't even blame her. I filed for divorce, but it turned out her knight in shining armor only wanted her as long as she was someone else's responsibility, and he dumped her soon after."

I winced, although I wasn't sure I had much sympathy for a woman who'd put that kind of pressure on Gabe. Especially back then.

"She killed herself. Overdosed on pills." His head hung low, and I drew myself up, wrapping a comforting arm around him.

"It was only then I realized she was mentally ill. I was too busy to see it."

I opened my mouth, then closed it again, needing to think how to approach this, to get him to understand and forgive himself. "You were too young, too busy, too … many things, I'm sure. But none of them means it was your fault. She needed help and never got it. It didn't begin when she married you, of that I'm certain."

He nodded. "I get that. Her mother admitted as much after the funeral. She thought marrying me would make her happy and take care of her issues."

I sighed. "It doesn't work that way. You're smart and you know this. Besides, look at the family you did raise. Look at Lucy and Decklan; they both got what they needed … thanks to you."

He shrugged. "I'm not sure I'll ever see it that way. After that, I closed myself off. Quick relationships, no feeling, no expectation. No one gets hurt. Then I saw you."

I blinked. Not once had I expected this to turn around back to me.

"You and that asshole at the country club. You had a white wine spritzer in your hand and a light blue dress that hugged your curves. I wanted you then. It was like some unseen force telling me you were it. Not to let you go. And every time I saw you with him … I couldn't breathe."

I couldn't breathe now.

As much as I knew there was instant attraction, to hear him acknowledge he had those same crazy feelings for me that I'd always had for him did something to me. It broke down my defenses, washed away any lingering anger at being manipulated, and put to rest my fear. This man who held himself responsible for everyone's well-being, everyone who mattered to him anyway, wouldn't control me or stifle me in any way. Well, in the bedroom, maybe—definitely—but I could handle that.

"Say something."

An unsure of himself Gabriel Dare was not a sight I appreciated. I ran a hand down his face, cupping his jaw. "You were it for me too. You are." I suspected he always would be.

He leaned down and kissed me, a brush over one side of my lips before moving to the other, then focusing on the center, sealing his mouth over mine. He kissed me over and over, his tongue sweeping inside and taking possession.

"You're mine, Iz," he said between kisses. "No arguments, no worrying about independence, money, working or not. We'll figure it out."

I opened my eyes, looking deeply into his dark blue ones. "I want kids one day," I said bravely. "I want the family I never had."

And, *oh God*, we hadn't used protection. Yes, we'd had the *I'm clean* conversation but not the *can you get pregnant* one. What was wrong with me? Thank goodness it wasn't the right time, but only idiots left things to chance.

My heart thumped in my chest. I didn't know what I was more nervous about, what I'd just said to him or what we'd done. As I held my breath, I realized the idea of a family wasn't something I'd compromise on.

"Frankly, I assumed Lucy and Decklan were all I'd have. That and my crazy cousins in Miami. But kids? With you?" His voice cracked with emotion, and I knew then everything would be all right. "Hell yes."

I jumped into his lap, and his strong arms came around me, holding me tight. "We didn't use protection," I reminded him.

"I can't bear to have anything between us."

I nodded in agreement. "It's really not the right time, but I have to get on the pill."

"Okay." He pressed a warm kiss to my lips. "But we're good?" he asked.

I smiled, feeling the sensation everywhere. "We're perfect. Thanks for telling me everything."

"Nobody else gets all of me. Only you." He brushed my hair off of my cheek. "I only expect one thing in exchange."

I raised my eyebrows. "What would that be?"

"All of you."

I shivered, knowing I'd given that to one man before. Or thought I had.

Gabe's hand slipped behind my neck, cupping me in a possessive grip. "Kitten?"

"You have me," I whispered.

He rose and kicked off his shoes and tossed his shirt onto a nearby chair. My eyes settled on his gorgeous bare chest, the dark sprinkling of hair that tapered into the waistband of his shorts, and the tented material bearing witness to his arousal.

That I understood. After our talk, knowing I had him in my life, a relationship that, though undefined, meant the world to me, I was also aroused. Memories of having him deep inside me caused my sex to clench and moisture to dampen my bathing suit. I squirmed in the chair.

He glanced my way and winked.

Before I could ask why, he scooped me up. With a squeal, I latched my arms around his neck. "Where are you going?" I asked, though, over my shoulder, I saw him edge closer to the beach and the gorgeous blue water lapping over the perfect sand.

"I need to cool off." He strode through the water, a man on a mission, only stopping when we were submerged. Warmth surrounded me, not just the water but the heat of Gabe's body.

Our bodies connected, my legs wrapping around his waist, my hot core rubbing against his hard length. "You're not helping me cool down," he said, sounding more playful than I'd ever heard from him before.

I actually thought Gabe was letting down walls, and I wanted to see more. I also wanted to play. "Maybe I want you hot." I leaned in and nipped at his earlobe.

A shudder racked his big body, and instinctively, I began rocking against him, pleasure consuming me.

He groaned and pulled the string on my bikini top, releasing the tie, and the suit fell to my waist. The warm sun hit my bare breasts, as strong as Gabe's always-intense gaze. He dipped his head and swirled his tongue around my breast and over my nipple, pulling on the tight bud with his tongue.

I arched my back, pushing myself closer, giving him more of me, and he took, lapping at my breast, nibbling and grazing my taut nipple with his teeth until I thought I'd come from those exquisite sensations alone.

As usual, he gave, but this time I wanted to return the favor, to make him feel as much as I did. He'd been solitary and alone for so long, and I wanted somehow to make him understand that he wouldn't be that way anymore. But he was intent on his task and held me to him in a way that didn't give me room to take over.

Suddenly he released my nipple with a pop. "You're not focused," he said in that dark, displeased voice that never failed to make me wetter and more aroused than I already was.

"I'm focused on figuring out how to make you feel as good as you're making me."

Instead of being pleased, he scowled. "Then I'm not doing enough to keep that busy mind of yours occupied."

"But—"

Without a word, he lifted me over his shoulder and carried me from the water. My bare breasts rubbed against his back, and despite my humiliation at his hold, I moaned at the erotic feeling.

Now I was more embarrassed than anything else. Damned frustrating man. "Gabe! Put me down!"

"Gladly." He deposited me back on the chair while releasing the last tie keeping my bikini top in place.

Suddenly my breasts were bare. Before I could cover myself, he grabbed both arms and tied them together with my bathing suit top, then raised them over my head. "Don't. Move."

His gaze came to my breasts, thrust forward by virtue of their position, and his eyes darkened with lust.

I swallowed hard. "Why?"

He raised an eyebrow. "Because you weren't getting the pleasure I intended for you to receive. You weren't paying attention. Now you have no choice."

"No, why do you tie me up?" I asked, really not understanding. Yes, it felt good. Yes, it forced me to think about nothing but every stroke of Gabe's tongue and the erotic things he did to my body. But his answer didn't make sense to me, and I wanted more. I wanted to know what went on inside his head. I'd only begun to get him to open up.

His greedy gaze roamed over me, and I *knew* my bikini bottoms would come off next. And he still hadn't answered me.

Warily, watching him the entire time, I lowered my hands—against his instructions. He reached out and tweaked my nipple hard. It hurt for an instant before blossoming into arousal, as evidenced by the moisture dampening my bathing suit.

I drew a shuddering breath. "Answer me, and I'll listen. And tack on an explanation for the need to cause a little pain with your pleasure while you're at it."

"Brat," he muttered. A grin tipped the edges of his sensual lips despite his best effort to remain serious.

"I need it, Iz. I need the control."

I got that much. "Why?" Everything inside me screamed it was more than an erotic kink, and I wanted to understand.

He exhaled hard. "I'm a caretaker."

"You were forced into the role when your parents died."

"It's just who I am. With other women, it was kink. With you, it's a driving, blinding need to give you pleasure at my hand. If you're tied, you have no choice but to give over to the pleasure." He paused.

And I rewarded his openness by lifting my arms back in place.

A blazing heat entered his eyes along with an appreciative smile on his lips. "It's simple," he went on. "If you argue or stop me like you did before, then I'm not doing my job, I'm not taking care of you. And make no mistake, kitten, I always intend to give you what you need. A little bondage, some light punishment, puts you back in the right headspace. That's it." He lifted his broad shoulders in a shrug. "It's all about you. It'll always be about you."

Liquid warmth oozed through my veins at his gruff admission. It wasn't just about kink, it was about me. *I* mattered. I couldn't remember when anyone had really cared about me before Gabe.

Tears threatened, and I struggled not to let them fall. Unfortunately, emotion got the best of me, and I choked back a sob. He was beside me in an instant, removing the ties to free my hands and pulling me into his arms, all thoughts of anything but comforting me forgotten.

Chapter Sixteen

Isabelle: Not All About Me

The rest of my time in Eden passed in a blissful blur. Work took up more time than I thought it would after realizing Gabe was on the island. To his credit, he really did let me have uninterrupted working hours with his sister. Today was our last day. Sadness engulfed me, but I'd always remember this island as the time I'd rediscovered Gabe and what it meant to really know someone and to care.

Lucy and I had agreed on one last meeting, and early morning, we sat in the basement at a table that had belonged to the original dance club, refining ideas. Lucy had brought sketches of her original vision, one based on the other Elite sites around the country. But considering this was an island that commanded an aura of mystery and respect, I suggested she veer off the expected course.

Elite was normally a glittery club that celebrities wanted to come to—people could see and be seen or request private space that normally consisted of a roped-off table or raised dais area where they could look out around the club—or have others see them and wonder just who they were. The island, on the other hand, was a place more for solitude and fantasy. I'd certainly gotten mine—Gabe luring me here, wanting me back, and giving me my dream job. I thought people who came to Eden would want something *more* for their private club.

I agreed that the main bar area should have the expected Elite feel, but I also suggested separate theme rooms that could be modified for different fantasies. Lucy loved the concept, and soon we were tossing around ideas that had us giggling and even squirming a bit when the Master stopped by and casually mentioned guests requesting BDSM-themed dungeons.

After taking notes, Lucy finally closed her portfolio and met my gaze. "Go find my brother, or he'll kill me for not giving him his final time with you here."

I smiled. "Thank you for everything. I know including me in this project was a favor, and I won't let you down." I rose to my feet.

"You aren't. You haven't. Your ideas are awesome."

Excitement and a sense of purpose filled me. I

picked up my bag, figuring I could run up to the room and see if Gabe and I could have some alone time before we had to leave the island. I turned to go.

"Iz—" Lucy had adopted Gabe's nickname for me.

I liked it. It made me feel like I had made a real friend, and I hoped she felt the same way. I turned back around. "What's up?" I asked.

"He'd kill me for talking about him again, but I need you to know, you changed him."

I narrowed my gaze.

"It's like he was walking around in this fog, dating women he couldn't possibly fall for, running the business, worrying about me … but never taking anything for himself. I worried he'd always be alone."

I swallowed hard, knowing what that was like and hating it for Gabe. Remembering the *other* room in his apartment, I knew Lucy was right. That was the exact path down which he'd been headed.

It was a path I knew too well. "I was the same way," I admitted to the other woman.

"Maybe you two saw that in each other. I don't know. But I do know you've changed him. He's more open and … vulnerable, not that he'd admit such a thing. But it's good. And it's thanks to you." Lucy stood and pulled me into a warm hug. "I like you, Iz."

Tears threatened. Other than Lisa, this was the first woman I'd felt a kinship with in years. "I like you too."

I didn't know what the future held for Gabe and me. It was too soon, things too fragile. But if I'd helped open him up and his sister noticed, that had to be a good thing.

Unfortunately, when I reached the room, Gabe was on a conference call with one of the managers at the New York hotel. He shot me a regretful look but did pull me into his lap while he spoke. He wrapped a solid arm around me and stroked my hair, all the while giving specific orders to the man at the other end.

I laid my head against his chest and thought about our time here. I now knew his favorite meals, what kind of fruit he liked—melons—and the kind he hated—pineapple. I'd learned he had had loving parents, which explained why I liked him and his siblings so very much. They'd done a great job. And I was sad they'd lost their mom and dad and wished I could have met them too.

And when Gabe ended the call, he immediately stripped off my pants, yanked his down, and soon I was easing myself onto him, taking him into my body the way he was already deep inside my heart.

Because I loved him, I thought, rocking myself against him, taking us both up and over quickly. I loved him, and I was sure this time.

Yes, it was fast.

Yes, it was furious.

And no, I didn't care.

* * *

Isabelle: Home

The trip home was a lot less frightening with Gabe and Lucy by my side. Even the small plane didn't scare me. I'd been gone for the long weekend, though it felt like much longer. Everything had shifted once again, only this time I felt much more in control.

Until we landed in New York.

No sooner had we exited the doors, following the driver who waited for us, than we were greeted by flashing cameras and people shouting questions.

"Mr. Dare! Is it true you're opening another club, this one on Eden?"

"Gabriel, did you see the Master of the island?"

"Who's the woman with you?" another one shouted.

I glanced up, taking in Gabe's unhappy scowl. "No comment."

I shivered, unused to being in the spotlight, and Gabe pulled me along, squeezing my hand tighter. He strode forward, but the vultures kept pace along with him.

"Who the hell alerted them?" he asked.

"It's good press for the clubs," Lucy said.

He didn't break stride until the driver stopped at the limo and opened the door for us to climb in.

Gabe waited until we were enclosed inside before he turned to his sister. "What the hell, Luce? Since when do I want to be ambushed?" he asked in a dangerous tone.

She merely shrugged. "This is the opportunity of a lifetime, Gabe. The club on Eden will be unlike any we've built before. I knew reporters would kill to have any tidbit of information, so I leaked the news that we'd be landing after a business trip. Relax and let me do my job."

He treated her to another scowl, then pulled me closer and stared out the window, his mood clearly soured. The car sped into Manhattan, and I stared out the window, wondering how things would change now that we were back in New York.

Since Lucy shared Gabe's apartment when she was in town, I expected the car to drop me at my place first. Instead, the limo headed farther uptown.

I cleared my throat. "Gabe, my apartment is downtown."

Lucy snickered.

Gabe inclined his head. "I'm aware of where you live, Isabelle. Tell me, did you plan to go home alone?" He leaned closer, his lips treacherously close to my ear.

"After all we shared, can you really sleep by yourself?"

His deep voice rumbled inside me, and I shivered at the warm breath of air across my skin, my body automatically reacting, my girl parts perking up.

"You're coming home with me," he said, as the car came to a halt in front of his building.

And that's how I moved in with Gabe. Lucy remained in the limo, having conveniently decided to stay with Decklan so she could have time with her other brother before returning to L.A. I knew Gabe well enough by now to know he'd sent her away so we could be alone.

I didn't feel too bad. Lucy was a woman with her own mind. If she wanted to stay, not even Gabe could drive her away.

I reentered Gabe's apartment, and to my surprise, though I'd only stayed there for a few days, I felt as if I'd returned home. It helped that the place smelled like Gabe, warm musk and all man, wrapping me in his strength. He paused in the kitchen, and out of habit, if I could form a habit in such a short time, I turned into my old room. At which point I found myself picked up and hauled over Gabe's shoulder and dumped on his big bed.

This time, it was all I could do not to laugh at his ridiculous overreaction. I sat up and scooted back against the pillows as he strode to the closets and began opening doors. "Your own closet. With all your clothes."

He gestured to the inside of a mini-room where familiar-looking clothes hung on matching hangers before moving across the room to a larger dresser and opening one drawer after another. "Personal items." He strode to the nightstand on the right side of the bed. "Your books and things. Want to see the bathroom next?"

I shook my head, mute. I couldn't think of a thing to say until the reality of how all this had occurred set in. "You sent someone into my apartment and moved out all of my things?"

He met my gaze, his unflinching, but I saw the stiff set of his shoulders, the near certainty I was about to flip out – and probably bolt.

"I moved you where you belong," he said tightly. "And before you give me a hard time, you should know that there's been no other woman in this bedroom. Ever."

I swallowed hard. No, I thought, they'd been in the separate room across the apartment. I knew what it meant that he'd moved me in here, understood the gesture for what it was—even if it had been high-handed and presumptuous.

If I'd been looking for something I could do for him, to let him know just how good he made me feel and how welcome, this was my chance.

I met his gaze, allowing an easy smile to cross my lips. "Did you remember my Tums?" I asked, which I realized I hadn't needed during my time on the island.

He grinned. "Night table drawer."

"Then I guess I've come home," I said with a tiny shrug of my shoulders.

His expression softened. "Now that that's settled, we didn't have a decent meal today. Are you hungry?"

"As a matter of fact, I am." I reached for the hem of my shirt and pulled it over my head. "Just not for food."

*   *   *

Isabelle: In Myself I Trust

Thanks to the waiting reporters, our return from the island had been captured by the *New York Post*, Page Six. I winced at the unflattering angle of myself in the lone photograph, not used to being the subject of public scrutiny. And thanks to the headline, I would be scrutinized and picked over. There were two mentions on the website, one about Elite, *Gabriel Dare to Open Club on Eden?*, and the other about his now apparently questionable single status, *Is One of New York's Most Eligible Bachelors No Longer On the Market?* And within the article, there was speculation on the curvaceous woman he kept protectively by his side. Yuck. What woman wanted to be referred to by her curves?

I slammed the laptop shut – a brand new laptop since Gabe hadn't liked the look of the used one I'd purchased on eBay after I started working for Lisa. I wasn't comfortable taking his gifts and money, still wondered what I could give back, but I accepted that *he* needed to do these things for me.

I did what I could. I made sure to be home in time to cook dinner, something I had always enjoyed doing for Lance, even when he hadn't appreciated it. There were times he wouldn't make it home for dinner, nor would he call to let me know. I'd merely package the meals and freeze them for another time. Times when I knew he wasn't coming home so I could eat them myself, because he didn't like frozen meals. I still didn't know how he knew the difference.

I shook off the past, reminding myself it was behind me. I was living a new life, one I loved. Working during the day, sometimes with Lucy by video or phone, sometimes with clients at Lisa's, home to cook during the week, and evenings with Gabe, reading in the library while he worked, or watching TV on the massive big screen in the family room, my head in his lap. Those nights, we would inevitably end up having sex on the couch, followed by more sex in his bedroom, which I'd begun to think of as ours.

Because amazingly, three weeks had passed since we'd reunited on Eden. I still woke up and wanted to pinch myself, but things were good. *I* was good. More importantly, *we* were good. I loved him, but I didn't say the words, having been burned before. It didn't escape my notice that neither had he.

And I knew that unless and until he did, I'd never be completely secure in the knowledge that I had his heart. And so I'd gotten myself on the pill, because until I was secure, a baby wasn't something I could risk.

* * *

Isabelle: Happy Birthday

I never told Gabe my birthday was coming. The day hadn't had any meaning in so long I rarely gave it much thought. So when I woke up to a warm tongue on my sex, Gabe's talented fingers parting my outer lips so he could delve deeper, it was, in fact, a morning like any other.

Welcome to my new world. I wasn't complaining.

Especially not when he slid his tongue deep inside me, setting off sparks that had my entire body trembling and on the edge of release. I raised my hips, rubbing myself against him until I exploded, moaning loudly, shaking as he kept me coming, replacing his tongue with his finger and curling it forward, hitting exactly the right spot.

I came harder, the sensations reaching every part of my body, ever-heightening waves consuming me. "Oh Gabe."

"I'm right here, kitten." Suddenly Gabe was over me, thrusting deep, hitting the same spectacular place inside me as his finger. But he was bigger, thicker, longer, and if I thought I'd shattered before, I was done for now.

"Keep coming for me," he said in a harsh voice.

I did. I was. My fingers curled into his back, gripping his skin, and he groaned, increasing the power of each deliberate thrust. It felt like heaven as he reached deeper, not just into my body but into my heart.

One final push and he came on a loud shout that sounded like my name, but I was still lost in sensation. Lost in Gabe. I wrapped my arms around him, holding his sweat-slickened skin as his harsh breathing rasped in my ear and his heavy body pressed me into the mattress. I struggled to breathe, not caring a bit.

Minutes later, our breathing still choppy, he did a slow roll to one side. "That was fucking fantastic," he muttered.

I couldn't help but grin. "Yeah, it was."

"Had to give you a birthday present to start your day." He pressed a lingering kiss to my lips.

"You know?"

He raised an eyebrow. "I know everything about you. Even the things you don't think are important enough to tell me." His tone told me he wasn't pleased by the omission.

I blinked in surprise. Then decided to give him more of me. "Has it escaped your notice that I've met your family and you haven't met mine?"

"Sally and Marvin Masters. College professors. Teachers," he said.

"They prefer the term *educators*," I said in a haughty tone.

Gabe sneered. "Cold-hearted individuals—"

"Who never meant to have a child," I said, reminding him of what had molded me into who I was.

"But they did, which meant they had obligations, and I'm not talking about the basics of food, clothing, and shelter."

I shrugged. "I realize now that their lack of warmth had me looking for it in the wrong places. I mistook what Lance offered for caring because I didn't know better." I shrugged and paused. "Maybe he did care in the beginning. I can't imagine I gave up my whole life for nothing, but he changed."

Gabe shrugged. "You know better now, kitten. You know exactly what it means to have someone care." He played with a lock of my hair, twisting it around his finger.

I smiled at that. "I do." I glanced at the clock, hating to interrupt our cuddling, but I knew his schedule. "You need to go, or you'll be late."

"They can't run the meeting without me."

I rolled my eyes. "Arrogant ass."

He grinned and levered into a sitting position, then pushed up from the bed. "Whatever works. See you home after work?"

I nodded, having a difficult time keeping my eyes on his face and not the rest of his spectacularly fine nude body.

He leaned down and kissed my nose. "No cooking. We're going out."

"But—"

He shook his head. "No buts. Your first real birthday celebration is going to be a special one." His dark blue eyes sparkled with delight—and an obvious plan.

The child in me, the one who'd never known a true celebration in her honor, lit up inside at the notion. "Whatever you say."

He laughed. "*That's* what I like to hear."

Chapter Seventeen

Gabe: "I take care of what's mine."

"I love a party!" Lucy said, striding around the room and checking decorations. "Gerbera daisies are my favorite. And these colors are spectacular!"

All Gabe knew was that there were red, orange, and yellow bouquets on each table and had matching balloons soaring from the middle.

"She's going to be so surprised," Lucy said.

"That's the plan." Gabe nodded to the bartender stocking the shelves before turning back to his sister. "You look beautiful," he told her, taking in the silver dress that, though too short, definitely added to her already-spectacular looks.

Her cheeks turned pink. "Thank you, big brother." She kissed his cheek. "And look! Decklan cleans up rather nicely too."

His brother wore black slacks and a white dress shirt, minus a tie, because heaven forbid Decklan should completely do as Gabe requested.

"I guess she's not such a stray," Decklan said, slapping Gabe on the back. "She must be here to stay for you to go to all this trouble."

Gabe glared at his brother.

"Shut up, Deck," Lucy said. "And don't bring up the whole arrest thing when you talk to Isabelle."

"Don't worry. Gabe's woman and I have an understanding now. She likes me since I brought her a present." Decklan grinned, causing Lucy to raise her eyebrows.

"What kind of trouble are you causing?" she asked.

Gabe rolled his eyes. "He bought her Tums. He aggravated her to the point where she needed antacids. He decides to call that a relationship. And we wonder why he doesn't have a woman in his life."

Lucy chuckled. Decklan, as usual, remained silent.

"Oh, people are starting to arrive," Lucy said, glancing toward the door.

"Seriously? You invited our whole crazy family? Have you lost your mind?" Decklan tipped his head toward the group who had just entered Elite.

First came what Gabe thought of as his original cousins, Ian and his pregnant wife, Riley, and Ian's siblings, Olivia, Avery, Scott, and Tyler.

Since it turned out that their father, Robert, had a second family on the side, Gabe, Lucy, and Decklan had discovered they had another set of cousins. And in walked Alex and his fiancée, Madison, and Alex's siblings, Jason, Samantha, and Sienna. Yes, Robert Dare was one fertile son of a bitch. But Gabe and his siblings didn't discriminate. Family was family, and over time and with effort, he'd gotten to know them all.

He greeted his cousins, thanking them for making the trip to New York and for arriving early enough to ensure a surprised guest of honor. Isabelle had her boss and her fiancé here, but there weren't many other people she'd befriended since leaving Lance.

Gabe intended to rectify that. He'd looked up old friends of hers who Lisa said Isabelle missed and invited them, hoping to reconnect her with her life. And to build one along with her. Which meant he'd invited his crazy Miami cousins.

He patted the box in his pocket. After all, they'd be her family too.

He excused himself to go pick up Isabelle for what she believed to be a romantic birthday dinner for two. He'd explain he needed to stop by the club for a few minutes on the way to the restaurant.

Surprise accomplished, he thought, pleased with his plan.

Chapter Eighteen

Isabelle: Surprise!

I rushed home from work to get ready for the evening. Gabe was due to pick me up after he wrapped up a meeting, then we'd head out to dinner. I showered, lathered up with moisturizer in the coconut smell he loved, and dressed in one of the summer outfits I'd bought for the island but hadn't gotten a chance to wear. I didn't have any special jewelry to put on—Lance had held on to everything—except the few things I'd bought for the trip, including the fake pearls.

I attached the clasp and fingered the delicate beading, my mind immediately returning to the moment Gabe had pulled me to the bedroom by the long strands. Along with the memory came the excitement I'd experienced at being with him again. The feeling hadn't waned, and I had the sense it never would.

I smiled to myself.

Since I had time, I decided to run down to the pharmacy on the corner and pick up a few items. I'd be back before Gabe arrived, and we were out of some necessities. The apartment was located conveniently to many places, and it didn't take me long to buy what I needed.

I approached the apartment building, preoccupied thinking about the night ahead, excited and anticipating a special evening.

"It's been a long time, Isabelle."

The familiar voice stopped me in my tracks. "Lance." I stared up at him, cursing at how he'd caught me off guard.

He looked the same, his blond hair perfectly cut, piercing blue eyes taking me in.

"Happy birthday, *darling*."

I narrowed my gaze, wondering what his agenda might be. "I'm surprised you remember. It's not like you bothered when we were together."

He'd managed to turn any birthday outings into business dinners, expenses he could write off. Early on in the relationship, he'd seemed contrite, like it was unavoidable. I realized later he just hadn't cared.

"Oh, come on. I always bought you expensive gifts."

I gritted my teeth, knowing he'd never understand

that those weren't the things that meant something to me. "Why are you here?" He'd clearly sought me out and had some sort of agenda.

"I wanted to congratulate you on landing another sugar daddy," he said with a sneer.

My hands curled around the brown bag. "You're a pig."

I no longer wondered what I had seen in him. Three months of self-reflection had taught me the answer. I'd seen what I wanted to see, what I'd desperately needed in my life at the time. I'd allowed myself to believe I was getting a man who loved me and, eventually, the family I wanted. I hadn't looked deeper at the man beneath the charming smile, and I'd paid the price.

I pushed past him, not wanting to listen to him further turn my relationship with Gabe into something cheap and meaningless.

He grabbed my arm hard enough to leave bruises. "What's the matter? The truth hurts?" he asked, spinning me around.

I swallowed hard, ignoring the painful jab at my self-esteem.

A quick glance around showed me the streets were quiet thanks to the heat wave suffusing the city. I couldn't make a scene, call attention to us, and get away.

"Why have you resurfaced now?" I asked, hoping the conversation would be brief.

"When that bastard Gabriel Dare pulled his accounts, he damaged my reputation within the firm. I couldn't do anything about it at the time." He flexed his hands, showing his impotence at Gabe's treatment. "At least when I heard you were struggling on your own, that gave me some satisfaction. It helped tide me over."

Nice, I thought. He was a real gentleman. I remained silent.

"But even Page Six picked up the new happy couple." He frowned now, the expression showing the real Lance, the unhappy, evil man who lived inside him. "Now you two are together, and his business is growing while I'm still trying to hold my portfolio of clients together and explain how I managed to lose the firm's biggest asset." Anger radiated from him in ugly waves.

"So?"

"So your birthday seemed like the best time to come wish you well. And to remind you that bottom-feeders like you inevitably end up alone."

I winced, unable to control my reaction to his words. Lance had always used words as weapons. Unfortunately, I knew from experience showing he'd hit his mark merely fed his appetite to spew more hateful things. I'd try to escape, but I didn't want him manhandling me again.

"Just how long do you think it will take before Gabriel Dare sees the real you? The pathetic gold digger who is so frigid in bed I had to turn to other women to get what I needed?"

Tears burned my eyes as every word hit its intended mark. I raised my chin, but I knew he wouldn't buy the unaffected act. But I wanted to be unmoved, and I reminded myself that Gabe wanted me.

But why? Your own parents didn't, a little voice in my head asked, one that sounded frighteningly like my own as a child. And one that reinforced Lance's words. Maybe he had a point. How long before Gabe grew bored, as Lance had? Before he cheated and humiliated me?

"Ahh, there they are." Lance swiped at the tears that had escaped down my cheek. "Proof you're still the same whiny bitch I remember. Not so sure of yourself anymore, are you? Sometimes it just takes a little reminder."

I treated him to a hate-filled glare. "You're a despicable excuse for a human being."

"And you're pathetic." He rolled his shoulders as if he hadn't a care in the world.

And now that he'd wounded me, maybe he didn't.

"Give your boyfriend my best," he said and, with

the smile he considered his most charming, strode off down the street, clearly pleased he'd just inflicted a deadly blow to my ego and self-esteem.

I raised a hand to my cheeks, coming away with black mascara streaks on my fingertips.

Knowing I couldn't let Gabe see me like this, I rushed back upstairs, ducking my head as I passed the doorman. I hoped to repair the outer damage. The inner pain would take longer to go away.

I looked into the mirror as I methodically cleaned the mascara and eyeliner smudges, redoing the entire mess with shaking hands. As I fixed my makeup, I couldn't help but remember Lance's hateful words, frowning at the images *gold digger* and *bottom-feeder* created.

I had left Gabe and the safety he'd offered me. I'd been determined to be independent. Granted, three months wasn't a lot of time to be on my own, but I hadn't caved and gone running back to a man, unable to make a fresh start. True, I'd been living in a friend's apartment, but I'd been paying rent, even if it had been below market value, along with utilities and expenses. Dammit, I'd tried. I was still trying. I had my own bank account, and I contributed to living here with Gabe—although I had to do it when he wasn't paying attention.

And if things with Gabe didn't work out for whatever reason, it wasn't like I didn't have the resources or the ability to start again.

I moved on to the lipstick and gloss, and when I was finished, I stepped back to look at the end result. Much better. If not for the painful knot in my stomach, I could almost believe the encounter with Lance hadn't happened.

But it had.

I groaned. "Are you really going to let stupid words and old insecurities send you running? For a third time?" I asked, taking in my reflection in the mirror.

"Running where?" Gabe appeared behind me.

I drew a deep breath and turned to face him. The scowl on his face told me he'd at least correctly interpreted the context of my statement, if not the reasons behind it.

He stepped forward, cupping my chin in his hand, tilting my head until I met his gaze. "I asked you a question."

I noted the muscle ticking in his jaw, reminded myself that *he'd* sought me out. Kept tabs on me while I'd carved out a life for myself. Wanted me for me.

And though he rarely showed them, he had vulnerabilities he'd let me see. "I'm not running anywhere," I assured him.

He studied me for a few more seconds, as if trying

to get into my head and see what he'd walked in on. Finally, he released me and stepped back. "But you thought about it?"

"For half a second, after—"

His gaze strayed from my face to my bare arm. "What the hell happened to you?" He lifted my hand, brushing fingers over the deep red indentations my ex had left on my arm.

I swallowed hard. "I had a run-in with Lance."

Heat flushed Gabe's cheeks. "I'll kill the son of a bitch."

As happy as I was that he was no longer focused on my running anywhere, I didn't want to have to bail Gabe out of jail. "He was just trying to upset me."

"And he did."

I sighed. "Because I let him get inside my head. Just for a few minutes. Maybe a little longer, but I pulled myself together. I'm good." Or I would be, I promised myself.

Gabe glanced at the bruising and frowned. "I'm not."

I stepped forward and wrapped my arms around his waist and laid my head against his chest. His solid body felt good against mine. He smelled like musk and man.

My man, I realized, and I wasn't letting go. "Better?" I asked.

He didn't answer.

So I tipped my head back. "Gabe?"

"What did he say that made me almost lose you?" he asked, his voice a tender mix of caring and frustration.

This was hard, mostly because it was an embarrassing statement of who I'd been. Or who Lance thought I'd been, which still held some amount of painful truth.

I inhaled a deep breath. "Basically, he called me a pathetic gold digger and said he'd had to turn to other women because I'm frigid in bed. Then he asked how long I thought it would be until you saw the real me and did the same thing." I looked away, rushing out the words, hoping that, once behind me, they'd lose impact.

They didn't. They still hurt, whether I believed them in my heart or not. "I should have left him much sooner. There wouldn't be any truth to his words if I had. Instead, I lived off of him even after I sensed things were over. And they should have been over."

"You trusted him."

I nodded. "He said he wanted me taking care of his home, that we'd have a family one day. I believed him. I honestly didn't realize how he'd isolated me from everyone or the lengths he'd gone to in order to ensure I had no one. I was a showpiece when he needed one, a glorified maid and all-around useless female when he didn't."

It hurt to admit those truths, but it was freeing in a way too. I glanced at Gabe. "Thank you," I whispered.

"For what?"

"For letting me go when I needed to. So I could come back when I wanted to. Even if you did set me up to get me here." I couldn't contain a smile.

"You were never really gone. Not from here." He touched his chest, above his heart. "I didn't expect to do this now," he said, more to himself than to me.

"I don't understand."

He cupped his hand around the back of my neck, and I sighed into him. I always felt so good when he took hold of me this way. "I love you, Iz."

I blinked, truly stunned. I'd hoped he did. It was everything I'd wanted him to say. Those three little words that set my heart soaring. "I love you too," I whispered.

The harsh lines of his face softened at my words. Those intense blue eyes warmed as he slid his hands from my neck. He now framed my face as he lowered his head and kissed me. Slowly, intently, and lovingly, this kiss wasn't all-consuming and hot, it wasn't about need or want. The sweet slide of his lips over mine said more than words. He told me I was special, the center of his world.

And he was mine.

He broke the kiss, and I watched, speechless, as he reached into his pocket and pulled out a jewelry box. A small, ring-sized jewelry box.

He popped the top open. "Marry me," he said. He didn't ask.

I trembled all over. And here I'd thought *I love you* was the greatest phrase I'd ever heard. Marry me? Cherry on top of an awesomely layered cake.

"Yes." I held out my shaking hand. I'd barely noticed the actual ring before he placed it on my finger. Nothing mattered but the meaning behind it.

Of course, when I really looked at the stone, the emerald shape covered my entire finger and then some. I couldn't begin to guess at the carat size, nor did I want to. "It's gorgeous," I managed to breathe out.

He shook his head. "You're gorgeous. It's just a diamond."

The tears that fell now were the good kind. The kind that indicated happiness and trust, that held the promise of the future I'd always dreamed of.

"I love you," I said, feeling the emotion with everything inside me.

"You do, huh?"

"Yeah."

"Then fuck the party," he muttered and lifted me into his arms, starting for the bedroom with a determined stride.

I clasped my hands around his neck, but his words hadn't escaped my notice. "Party?" I repeated.

"Ahh, hell," he muttered. "My entire family and our friends are waiting at Elite. We're already late."

My heart began a steady pounding. "You arranged a surprise party for me?"

He inclined his head. "I was going to propose there."

I clasped his cheeks and kissed him again, sliding my tongue inside his hot, waiting mouth, but it didn't last long. Gabe broke the kiss, looked at me, and groaned. "We have to get to the club."

I brushed my hands through his hair, feeling the soft strands beneath my fingertips. "I know." Unable to help myself, I nipped the side of his jaw, feeling playful and pleased. I'd conquered my insecurity and fear—okay, well, I still had some work to do on those things—but my reward for trying was fantastic.

Gabe's fingertips bit into my waist. "You're testing my restraint, kitten. But if we're going to attend this thing, we have to go."

I nodded. "One sec." I dabbed at his lips with my fingers, wiping off traces of my lipstick. "All better. You can let me go now."

He shook his head. "Never ever again."

I smiled because Gabe never said what he didn't mean.

Chapter Nineteen

Gabe: Invitation to Eden

Gabe loved this island. There was the privacy—they were alone on a stretch of endless white sand and clear blue water. There was the mystery—his entire family and many friends were here for the opening of Elite, and yet there was no one around to hear or see a thing. And there was the view—his wife in a red bikini, showing off her luscious curves.

So much had changed in a short time. Trust between them had blossomed. When he'd rescued her from the police station, he'd thought she was the one who'd needed to let down her walls. In the time since, she'd showed him trust ran two ways. Together they were creating a life, in more ways than one.

He had someone to come home to at night, who made sure he didn't get lost in work, not that he could with her waiting at the end of the day. He had an equal partner in day-to-day living. He shared his highs and the lows—to his surprise, Isabelle was interested in his business frustrations. Before her, he'd mull them over all night and return to them again in the morning. These days, they talked, he let his day go, and then he took her to bed.

He wouldn't have thought interior design was his thing, but he enjoyed the stories she had about annoying clients and stubborn people. Most of all, he was proud of her successes, this club opening on Eden being the biggest of all.

For so long, he'd closed himself off to the possibility of love and a future because one woman had instilled him with fear and the possibility that he couldn't be enough or do enough. With Isabelle, there was always more he wanted to give. It always gave him pleasure to do things for her, to take care of her in small but important ways.

Like making sure her bastard ex was fired from his job for attempting to poach clients and embezzling funds. Gabe hadn't known what Daltry was up to, but a snake like Lance had to be doing something to regain his former golden boy status on Wall Street. All Gabe had had to do was hire a private detective and wait for the evidence, then let the bastard bury himself. Now the SOB was too busy trying to stay out of jail to think about anyone but himself.

Gabe watched with pleasure as Isabelle walked the beach, her hand on her stomach. He grinned, fully aware she had no idea she was pregnant. She'd been so busy getting ready for the opening of Eden Elite, first in New York and then here, she didn't remember to eat meals unless he reminded her, let alone take her pill. He hadn't realized until it was probably too late to do anything about it, and he really hadn't wanted to.

Lately, there were times she was queasy, which she blamed on nerves. Adding in the subtle differences in her body, he knew better. Her breasts were more sensitive, her stomach a tiny bit rounder. She cried when she was happy and also when she was sad. More than usual. It wasn't like he knew the signs, but he did remember his cousin Ian mentioning the changes in his own wife in the early stages of her pregnancy. Ian and Riley now had a baby girl, who Gabe felt fairly certain would turn her father's hair prematurely gray. The uptight bastard deserved it, Gabe thought, laughing.

But thanks to them, he knew Isabelle most probably was carrying their child. When this club opening was over, he intended to tie her to their bed and keep her there for the next nine months. Okay, true, she wouldn't allow it, but he was pretty sure she'd let him use the ties when it counted, he thought.

On the heels of that image, Isabelle trussed up and spread, waiting for him to bury his cock deep inside her, he strode down to the beach, wrapping his arms around her waist and resting his chin on her shoulder. "Hey, kitten."

She spun in his arms, aligning their bodies with a sigh. "Happy three-month anniversary," she said again, having woken him up with those words this morning.

As if he'd forget. He'd hauled her off to Vegas, his brother and sister in tow, and married her three months after they'd gotten engaged. Waiting wasn't his style or in his vocabulary.

"Happy anniversary." He nuzzled her neck, enjoying the coconut scent of suntan lotion and Isabelle. "How are you feeling?" He gingerly palmed her stomach.

"So-so. I'll be glad when this opening's over. Nerves and all that."

He bit back a grin. "Everything ready for tonight?" he asked.

She nodded. "Nothing out of place, no stone unturned."

"Will Lucy notice if you're a no-show?" He slid his hand down the front of her bikini bottoms, gliding his fingers over her damp lower lips.

She moaned her appreciation. "Yes, and so will I. I worked too hard for this to miss the main event."

"Knew that," he muttered. "And I want to be by your side when you collect all the accolades for how the club turned out." He continued to play with her pussy, knowing he could give her one good orgasm before she had to shower and get ready for the night. He'd get his treats later on.

"It's Lucy's baby," Isabelle reminded him, still thinking about the club, but she began rocking her hips against his hand.

Another thing Gabe loved about Isabelle, her lack of ego or need to brag. That was fine; he could brag enough for them both. And Lucy planned to share credit.

"It's good that you know that," he told her. "Because you're going to be too busy with *our* baby to worry about club openings." He hadn't planned on telling her, but now seemed as good a time as any. He slid his hand from her bottoms and waited for the reaction.

Her mouth opened then closed again. "What are you talking about?" she finally asked.

"I think you're pregnant, kitten."

"I can't be!"

"No? Queasy? Check. Sore boobs?" He gently rubbed his finger over her nipple, and she squirmed out of reach. "Check. Where are your pills? Or should I ask, when was the last time you took one?"

The ocean waves were the only sound as she thought back. "Oh my God."

He enclosed his hand protectively around her belly.

"Oh my God," she said again. "I'm… We're… Are you…?"

"Ecstatic, baby. You?" Suddenly he was the nervous one. Maybe she loved the job so much that kids weren't something on her radar now. Maybe she no longer wanted the family she'd thought she did. What if—

"Oh my God!" she exclaimed yet again, and before he knew what was happening, she was in his arms, legs wrapped around him, peppering kisses all over him.

The twisting around his heart eased. Nothing had changed, after all. She was still a woman with an unloved little girl inside her, who wanted nothing more than a family to call her own.

He wanted nothing more than to give it to her, and he hoped that he had.

"Do you think they have home pregnancy tests on this island?" she asked.

"To hear the stories, some pretty amazing things have happened here. I think one phone call can get you anything you need."

"Rumor has it it's the Bermuda Triangle nearby that makes the island experience so different for everyone."

He laughed. "Every time I wonder how the hell we're so alone and isolated with my entire family supposedly nearby, I think the same thing."

Isabelle rolled her eyes. "Let's go make that phone call. I want to know for sure."

"Doesn't matter. If you're not pregnant yet, I'll just spend all my free time making sure that you are." Now that he knew what it felt like to hope, to want their child, to know she did as well, on the off chance he was wrong, he was damned determined to make it happen.

He started for the room, Isabelle still in his arms.

"About that little comment you made? The one about me not having time for club openings because of our baby?" She tipped her head back, looking at him.

He nearly tripped. The last thing he needed was her flipping out on him, thinking he wanted to take everything she'd worked for away from her. "I was joking, Iz. You can work if that's what you want."

Although he'd love it if she stayed home with the baby. His mom had done that. But he knew how important Isabelle's independence was to her. It was the one thing she'd fought him for—the only thing. And he wouldn't risk losing her by putting that at risk.

She bit down on her lower lip, and he slowed to a

stop, keeping her close to him. "What if I don't?" she asked.

"What?"

"Want to work? What if I want to be home for the baby? I mean, I can do some consulting work with Lucy, I guess, to keep my hand in things so I have something for me … but…" She drew a deep breath.

He waited. Everything he was—everything he cared about—was tied up in this woman. He'd give her the moon if that's what she wanted.

Her eyes grew glassy. "All I ever dreamed of was having a family that was mine. People who loved me, who I loved, who appreciated one another, including their kids. Everything I never had growing up."

She placed a hand over her stomach, and he covered her hand with his.

"That's why I gave up everything for Lance, and when that turned out to be an illusion, like my childhood was, I was determined to know I could stand on my own. You gave me that." Her smile lit up his world. "And even though it's the antithesis of everything I told myself I needed, I just want to be home with any kids that we have. Because I love you, but more important, I trust you."

Damn, but she undid him.

He lowered her to her feet, slid his hand behind her neck, and pulled her in for a long kiss. "I love you,

Iz."

"I love you too. Now let's go see if we can't get me one of those tests."

He grabbed her hand, and together they made their way back to the suite, the same one they'd stayed in the first time. And there, on the baby grand piano, was a bucket of apple cider and, beside it, an early home pregnancy test.

The note read: Welcome to Eden, where reality is whatever you wish it to be.

Carly Phillips

Book 1 in the Dare to Love series, Riley & Ian's story, DARE TO LOVE and book 2, DARE TO DESIRE are available NOW!

Dare to Touch – Olivia Dare's story will be available sometime in Fall 2014.

Like what you just read? Make sure to check out the rest of Invitation to Eden series. Sign up for our mailing list (http://eepurl.com/QvEdn) to receive new release alerts!

For more information about the island of Eden, check out our website!
http://www.invitationtoeden.com/

Have you read Invitations to Eden's other July releases?

Ivy in Bloom (Hothouse #2) by Vivi Anna writing as Tawny Stokes

After getting out of a bad relationship and dropping out of university, Ivy Watts decides she needs some much needed stress therapy. So when she discovers her parents have been invited to a luxury private island resort called Eden, she manages to finagle herself her own invitation. She expects to laze around on the beach with a drink in her hand and figure out what she wants to do with the rest of her life, but what she doesn't expect is to learn a few life lessons from the tall, dark, older handsome man in the penthouse suite.

Second Glances (The Springs series) by Elena Aitken

When Kylie Wilson receives a mysterious invitation for an all expenses paid trip to a tropical, all inclusive resort, there's no doubt in her mind who it came from—Marcus Stone, the only man she's ever really loved. The same man who'd promised her forever and then promptly left town to pursue his dream without so much as a backward glance. Kylie owes it to herself to take a chance, and despite her conflicted feelings, she decides to risk her heart again and is soon jetting toward the island of Eden and the man she hopes will finally fill the void in her life. But when she arrives, all is not as she expected it to be. More to the point, *he* is not who she expected him to be. And on an island that is supposed to *'know exactly what you need'*, can Kylie open her body, mind, and more importantly—her heart to someone and something, she's never considered?

ALL EDEN RELEASES:

March

Master of the Island by Lauren Hawkeye

April

Random Acts of Fantasy by Julia Kent

Yours Truly, Taddy by Avery Aster

Escape From Reality by Adriana Hunter

May

Hydrotherapy by Suzanne Rock

Fight For Me by Sharon Page

June

Breaking Free by Cathryn Fox

Hold Me Close by Eliza Gayle

Queen's Knight by Sara Fawkes

July

Dare to Surrender by Carly Phillips

Ivy in Bloom by Vivi Anna writing as Tawny Stokes

Second Glances (The Springs) by Elena Aitken

August

Rough Draft by Mari Carr

Blurring The Lines by Roni Loren

Return to Sender by Steena Holmes

September

Pleasure Point by Eden Bradley

Wild Ride by Opal Carew

Master of Pleasure by Lauren Hawkeye

October

Her Desert Heart by Delilah Devlin

The Capture by Erika Wilde

Thorne of a Rose by Kimberly Kaye Terry

November

Falling or Flying by R.G. Alexander

Elusive Hero by Joey W. Hill

Captive of Desire by Sarah Castille

December

Delicious and Deadly by C.C. MacKenzie

Pleasure Games by Jessica Clare

How To Tempt A Tycoon by Daire St. Denis

Thank you so much for reading Isabelle and Gabe's story. I would appreciate it if you would help others enjoy this book, too. Please recommend to friends and leave a review when possible!

Stay up to date with what's happening with Carly's books by visiting these links:

My website:
www.carlyphillips.com

Sign up for Carly's Newsletter:
http://www.carlyphillips.com/newsletter-sign-up/

Sign up for Blog and Website updates at:
http://www.carlyphillips.com/blog

Sign up for Text Updates of New Releases:
http://tinyurl.com/pbq4fbx

Carly on Facebook:
www.facebook.com/CarlyPhillipsFanPage

Carly on Twitter:
www.twitter.com/carlyphillips

Follow or Friend me on Goodreads:
www.goodreads.com/author/show/10000.Carly_Phillips

CARLY'S MONTHLY CONTEST!

Every month I run a contest at my website – Visit: http://www.carlyphillips.com/newsletter-sign-up/ and enter for a chance to win a $25 gift card! You'll also automatically be added to my newsletter list so you can keep up on my newest releases!

About the Author

N.Y. Times and *USA Today* Bestselling Author Carly Phillips has written over 40 sexy contemporary romance novels. After a successful 15 year career with various New York publishing houses, Carly made the leap to Indie author, with the goal of giving her readers more books at a faster pace at a better price. Carly lives in Purchase, NY with her family, two nearly adult daughters and two crazy dogs who star on her Facebook Fan Page and website. She's a writer, a knitter of sorts, a wife, and a mom. In addition, she's a Twitter and Internet junkie and is always around to interact with her readers.

CARLY'S BOOKLIST by Series

Below are links to my series on my website where you will find buy links for each novel!

Dare to Love Series

http://www.carlyphillips.com/category/books/?series=dare-to-love

Dare to Love

Dare to Desire

Dare to Surrender

Serendipity Series

http://www.carlyphillips.com/category/books/?series=serendipity-series

Serendipity

Destiny

Karma

Serendipity's Finest Series

http://www.carlyphillips.com/category/books/?series=serendipitys-finest

Perfect Fit

Perfect Fling

Perfect Together

Serendipity Novellas

http://www.carlyphillips.com/category/books/?series=serendipity-novellas

Kismet

Fated

Hot Summer Nights (Perfect Stranger)

Bachelor Blog Series

http://www.carlyphillips.com/category/books/?series=bachelor-blog-series

Kiss Me If You Can

Love Me If You Dare

Lucky Series

http://www.carlyphillips.com/category/books/?series=lucky-series

Lucky Charm

Lucky Streak

Lucky Break

Ty and Hunter Series

http://www.carlyphillips.com/category/books/?series=ty-hunter-series

Cross My Heart

Sealed with a Kiss

Hot Zone Series

http://www.carlyphillips.com/category/books/?series=hot-zone-series

Hot Stuff

Hot Number

Hot Item

Hot Property

Costas Sisters Series

http://www.carlyphillips.com/category/books/?series=costas-sisters-series

Summer Lovin'

Under the Boardwalk

Chandler Brothers Series

http://www.carlyphillips.com/category/books/?series=chandler-brothers-series

The Bachelor

The Playboy

The Heartbreaker

Stand Alone Titles

http://www.carlyphillips.com/category/books/?series=other-books

Brazen

Seduce Me

Secret Fantasy

Love Unexpected Series

http://www.carlyphillips.com/category/books/?series=ebooks

Perfect Partners

Solitary Man

The Right Choice

Midnight Angel

Anthologies

http://www.carlyphillips.com/category/books/?series=anthologies

Truly Madly Deeply (boxed set of Perfect Partners, The Right Choice, Solitary Man)

Sinfully Sweet (also includes The Right Choice and 5 other authors)

More Than Words Volume 7

Santa Baby (Carly's Naughty or Nice novella)

Invitations to Seduction (Carly's Going All the Way – not in print)

Made in the USA
San Bernardino, CA
28 August 2014